Cobalt City

Dark Carnival

Timid Pirate Publishing

Nathan Crowder, Editor

Direct all orders to:
Timid Pirate Publishing
509 N. 85th St. #14,
Seattle, WA 98103
www.timidpirate.com

ISBN 978-0-9830987-6-8
Printed in the United States of America
Timid Pirate Publishing: October, 2011

Table of Contents

Introduction

In the world of tent-based entertainment, there are the traveling circuses, the county fairs, and the carnivals. Growing up in small-town Colorado, I got plenty of the first two, but the carnival is another beast entirely. See, a circus has the big tent with shows, while a fair has some rides and games along with livestock and crafts showings (at least all the ones I've gone to). But a carnival has a bit of both, along with something relegated to our dark, collective past—the sideshow.

I don't know if I've ever been to a real carnival, but it feels like I have. Between Bradbury's *Something Wicked This Way Comes*, the movie *Freaks*, Katherine Dunn's *Geek Love*, and the lamentably short-lived HBO series *Carnivale*, I think the seed has been planted in my subconscious. There is something magical, mysterious, perhaps a bit dark and dangerous about the shadowed midway. The carnival is the allure of the road, misfits and freaks, secret rites and rules cloaked beneath greasepaint, chipped paint, and gaudy canvas. For those of us who never quite fit in, it is a traveling company of our own kind—or one where we wish we belonged.

At Timid Pirate Publishing, we had a random conversation one September night in 2010 about the carnival as we prepped Cobalt City *Timeslip* for printing. We had been discussing options for the next anthology. See, it turns out that one of us had recently had an intense dream about a Cobalt City anthology that centered on a dark carnival. That brought up two immediate thoughts: "Aren't all carnivals dark?" and "What a fun idea!"

All our authors had to work with was the character information provided online, and a very rough description of Le Carnaval Pomme D'or—little more than the names of some of the personnel. There were so many ways this enterprise could have failed. We could have had numerous wildly divergent visions of the carnival come in that would have to be rectified. We could have had thirty submissions all featuring the same character.

Instead, the Dark Carnival took shape before our very eyes. With the Haunted Tunnel of Love in Rosemary Jones' "Fortunes for the Brave Heart," the hall of mirrors in Erik Scott de Bie's "Funhouse," and the malevolent Ferris wheel in Dawn Vogel's "Unexpected Sparx," the attractions came to life—sometimes literally. The personnel came out of the shadows with the ringmaster in Amber Keller's "Now You See Me, Now You Don't," the 8th wonder of the world Iboni and her mother in "Custody Battle" by Charlie Kenmore, while the big top got a big magic show courtesy of Matt Adams and "Harrigan the Magnificent," and aerialists swung among the spotlights thanks to Ashley Bates and "Dance With the Devil." Even carnival food put in a timely appearance with Catherine and Andrew Warren's Knockabout story "Call & Response" and Jeremy Zimmerman's Snowflake magnum opus "Snowflake's Chance in Hell." And the dark roots of the carnival were explored by Minerva Zimmerman in "Apples & Arrows" and in a final climax story joint-written by several of the contributing authors called "Carnival Heart."

What began as a nightmare became a dream—a malevolent carnival that would test the super-heroes of Cobalt City to their breaking point. And I couldn't be happier.

So fasten the safety bar. Keep your arms and legs inside at all times. Le Carnaval Pomme D'or is not responsible for lost items or souls.

Let's get the ride started.

Nathan Crowder
September 2011

Apples & Arrows
Minerva Zimmerman

There was no desire in Aiko's heart. It sat numb in his chest as he opened the mail—mostly bills and purchase orders. He turned a black envelope over and pushed the phone intercom for the front counter.

"Outrageous Fortune," said a high lilting male voice, "your desires are our business."

"Cleo," Aiko said, sliding the arrow-shaped letter opener under the envelope flap. "Do we have door prizes for Fetish Night?"

A rhythmic tapping sound on the other end of the phone meant Cleo was flicking his tongue piercing against his teeth. Lucky for Cleo, Aiko provided excellent dental coverage.

Aiko pulled an over-sized carnival ticket out of the envelope. His fingers ran over the gilt lettering that read, "Le Carnaval Pomme D'or" and the embossed golden apple in the center of the ticket. Aiko bit his lip and tried to ignore the feeling that blossomed in his chest.

"Looks like we have some DVDs, pocket vibrators, and a whole slew of novelty condoms and lube set aside for it," said Cleo after a slight pause.

"Would you also pick out a few of the more popular items?" Aiko took a lighter out of his desk and set the ticket on fire. The flames curled the fancy paper to ash as Aiko dropped it towards the wastebasket.

"How many? Just a sec." Cleo moved the phone away from his face and his voice was muffled like the phone was pressed against his shoulder. "Welcome to Outrageous Fortune, is there something I can help you gentlemen find?"

Aiko couldn't hear the customer's reply, but he heard Cleo's sharp breath and saw the panic light glow red on the intercom before Cleo said, "Excuse me," into the phone and hung up.

Aiko flipped on the surveillance monitors behind him while he dialed security.

"This is Jackson," said the deep voice on the other end of the phone. "We're moving into position."

"Two men," said Aiko flipping through the various cameras on the monitors. "One at the counter and one pretending to look at DVDs. I'm heading down."

"Affirmative," said Jackson.

Aiko slipped a black velvet jacket over his unbuttoned burgundy shirt. He grabbed dark sunglasses from the desk and mussed his bleached hair. It wasn't quite noon yet and he had a reputation to uphold.

Owning a thriving and visible business in The Hollows had its little hiccups, like when the Blow Monkey Gang decided to push for protection money. It happened often enough there was a procedure in the employee handbook:

-Be polite
-Alert security
-Let Aiko handle it.

He swooped down the steps and stood in the secure passage between Outrageous Fortune and Quiver, the nightclub he owned next door. All of the doors in and out of this passage were keycoded. Only Aiko and three others had codes.

He punched his code into the keypad and did his best to look tired and hungover as he slouched into the bright lights of the adult superstore.

"Tell me there's coffee." Aiko staggered towards the counter.

"Sorry," said Cleo. "I could get you a latte?"

"Latte yes." Aiko pulled up a stool and curled his bare toes around its footrest. "Big one."

"You're the boss." Cleo slipped past the men and down the street toward Ares Coffee.

"Perhaps you can help us," said one of the men stepping forward.

Aiko rested his head on the counter and looked up at the man like it took great effort. "Likely, as I doubt you can help me."

"Excuse me?" The man took a step back.

"I," said Aiko, "can offer you many things. But you have nothing I need, want, or fear."

The man's hand went unconsciously toward the gun in his waistband. "What do you mean?"

Aiko sat up and looked at the man over his sunglasses. "You came here looking for money, but that's not what you really want. I can give you your heart's desire." He let his feet alight on the cool linoleum floor. "Step into the office." He gestured at the open office door.

The second man started to follow the first.

"Stay here," said the first.

"Whatever you say, Van."

Aiko staggered and put a hand against the counter, resting his forehead against the countertop like he was trying not to hurl. His other hand slid underneath and scrawled a quick note, *Do nothing.*

He lifted his head off the counter and smiled weakly at the two men. "Fetish Night at Quiver tonight. You should come. We have plenty of clothing in stock." He gestured at the racks of rubber, vinyl and leather.

Van let his disgust show. "Not interested."

Aiko gave an exaggerated shrug while flicking fingers to the second man and then put a hand to his head like the movement had been painful.

"Late night?" asked Van.

"No," said Aiko. "Morning came too early." He teased out the thread of desire dangling off Van.

3

Aiko smiled. Yes, he could work with this. He sat down at Cleo's desk and motioned for Van to close the door.

"What do you mean desire?" asked Van. "You gonna offer me hookers from the back?"

"No." Aiko picked up the phone. He reached back along the thread for the bit of info he needed. "You don't care about sex. There's only one person you care about." He started dialing the phone.

"What are you talking about? How do you know that?"

The phone was ringing on the other end. Aiko handed it to Van and closed his eyes to focus on feeding the desire in the man's heart.

Van stopped breathing when someone picked up.

Aiko opened his eyes. There were tears streaming down Van's face.

"Mama?" Van wiped away the tears. "Slow down. I can't understand. No, I'm not dead."

Aiko wrote "You'll see her soon" on a post-it and handed it to him.

"I'll…I'll see you soon Mama. I gotta go now." Van paused. "Love you too."

Aiko took a car key out of the desk and laid it in front of Van. He opened the back door. "There's an unregistered blue sedan in spot C47 in the parking garage. Take it. Don't stop until you're far from here. Go home."

"I…I can't."

Aiko crossed the room and placed a hand on Van's chest amplifying the longing within. "You can."

Van took the key. "Thank you."

Aiko closed and locked the garage access door. He sighed and straightened the purchase orders on Cleo's desk. Once, a job well-done would have given him a sense of satisfaction, now it was simply a means to an end. He got no joy from it.

Aiko walked back out into the store. Jackson and Cleo were the only ones there.

Jackson gestured outside. The second man was getting into his car.

Cleo handed Aiko a "guerra-sized" cinnamon latte. "Said he had to ask his girlfriend an important question. Couldn't wait."

"I think that went well." Aiko took a sip. "Did you get those door prizes picked out?"

That night, Aiko floated across the dance floor. He could feel the vinyl of his tight bondage pants squeak in protest and the dangling hardware clink against each other as he moved. The pulsing music reverberated under his bare feet. He smoothed his hands down the red birds embroidered on the black silk halter top that covered his chest but left his arms and back bare. Two small wings were tattooed over his shoulder blades—too small for angel wings—like wings of a bird, each feather delicately shaded into his flesh and highlighted with white ink that shone against his fawn-colored skin.

He let the desires of the crowd roll over him like lapping waves. He knew them all—every heart's desire of Cobalt City. He stretched his arms over his head and undulated to the music, his fingertips purposefully flicked towards those around him as he danced towards the bar.

No one left Quiver alone unless they wanted to.

The club was crowded. Probably a line outside. Aiko hadn't bothered to check the exterior cameras before making his entrance. He smiled at the leather-clad couple who'd just walked in the door. Both maintained individual memberships at the highest level the club offered: unrestricted access and guaranteed privacy. They had enough secrets between and about them to fill a library. He sucked and bit his lower lip. Aiko enjoyed herding those particular cats. Those two, had complicated desires.

There weren't any seats available at the bar. He touched the Celtic-tattooed shoulder of a girl sitting alone.

"I'm Aiko," he said stretching his lips in a slow, confident smile.

"Isn't that a girl's name?" she asked over the music.

He leaned in closer, his lips nearly brushing her ear. "Why? Do you want to tie me in corsets and dress me in skirts?"

She closed her eyes and swallowed hard.

He trailed a finger down her arm. "Not tonight, sweet girl." He tilted her head and flicked a finger towards a slim youth flailing on the dance floor. "There."

The youth looked up suddenly, like he'd been struck. He saw the girl and smiled.

She got up and the two moved towards each other.

Aiko slid into the girl's seat and sipped the pomegranate martini the bartender had waiting for him.

A fight broke out at the other end of the bar. Aiko raised a finger to quell it—and stopped, confused. There was no desire in the fighters' hearts.

He scanned the room. A man in white leather with long black hair perched on the edge of one of the dance platforms staring at Aiko. Aiko stared back, as a stab of guilt iced through his chest. The man's face mirrored Aiko's own.

"Brother." Aiko's whisper was lost beneath the music.

His brother cocked a finger gun at Aiko and mock-fired.

Aiko was off his chair and half-way across the room before his brain brought him to a skidding halt. What was he doing? He looked towards the dance platform, but his brother was already moving across the club, white leather jacket disappearing into the members-only entrance.

Aiko slipped between the curtains and into darkness. He expected a punch, a blade in the ribs—something. There was no one there and nowhere to go but down.

"As above, so below" read the phosphorescent lettering above his head as he descended the stairs. People could pretend this was another world all they wanted. It didn't make it the truth. Glow tape outlined the edge of the steps so no one stumbled. There was an elevator too, but for security reasons it only carried passengers up, never down.

Jackson and Donovan stood on either side of the door at the bottom of the stairs.

"Boss?" asked Jackson.

"Did someone just come through here?" Aiko tried to cast his senses outward, searching for his brother. For the absence of desire. "White leather jacket?"

"Not in the last ten minutes, and no white jackets." Jackson frowned. "You want us to go look?"

Aiko forced a smile and adjusted the hair around his ear with a finger. "No. It's fine."

"You OK, boss?" Jackson's squared features wrinkled in worry. It made him look like an over-grown eight-year-old. "Heard there was a fight upstairs."

"A scuffle, easily dealt with." A more genuine smile spread on Aiko's face. Jackson's concern was touching. "I'm fine. Just tired."

Aiko waved his left wrist at the RFID sensor to unlock the door between the two large men. The black silicone bracelet key passes were incredibly popular—easy to keep track of and sort of a secret symbol. Many members wore them outside the club. Aiko didn't, but as Porn Prince of Cobalt City, he didn't need a secret method of expressing his hobbies. It was written in neon on the side of the building.

The latch clicked and Donovan opened the door. Aiko was always struck by the smell of the dungeon. His employees cleaned, disinfected and sterilized the space after every use but a musky human smell persisted over the smell of bleach and vinegar.

A red curtain partitioned the doorway from the rest of the space. Aiko took a deep breath and sent tendrils of expectation curling around the occupants before he tossed it back and strode into the room with a movie-star swagger.

His brother wasn't here. The dim flame of hope guttered and died in his chest.

Several knots of regulars milled around the few occupied apparatus or lounged on sofas. Some were here to watch, some to play. It was early. Most of the members were still upstairs or had yet to arrive.

Aiko wasn't going to wait. He was here to put in appearance. He glided around the room nudging couples towards one another or igniting desire between partners. He was tired and upset, but it was important members had a magical night.

A lone female sub sat alone in a corner, no Master or Mistress purposefully ignoring her.

"Come with me," he ordered her. He slipped an arm possessively around her and waited for anyone to challenge his claim. None did.

She stood meekly beside him, hope and longing blossoming within. Desire for attention so fierce it'd leave marks on more than just skin. Another time Aiko might have fulfilled that desire himself.

Not tonight.

He felt the room again. No one had claimed her, but there was one who longed for her. Strove to be worthy of a depth of devotion like hers. Aiko grabbed the thread of desire and pulled. A soft middle-aged man with lonely eyes came forward. Well, he wasn't going to grow Aiko's reputation, but one had to keep everyone off balance somehow.

"Follow me," he told them and strode for the elevator with deliberate purpose. When all three were safely inside and between floors, Aiko paused the elevator. Blonde hair cascaded to her shoulders and framed the crimson collar at her throat. He slipped his hands around her waist and stroked the sides of her crushed velvet bodysuit. "You've pleased me greatly," he whispered into her ear. He pulled her against his body and locked eyes with the man over her head.

The pulse at the man's graying temples was quick and visible.

"You will earn her devotion tonight," Aiko whispered.

He touched both at once and stepped back as they suddenly found in each other what they'd been longing for.

Aiko pushed a series of buttons and flicked on the intercom. "Have a car meet us in the garage."

"Sure thing, boss," replied a static-distorted voice.

The elevator resumed its ascent. The doors opened into a small lobby in the parking garage next to Quiver. The garage was how he made a good portion of his money. He advertised $1 cover for Quiver on Friday and Saturday, free for members—but being in The Hollows, people didn't want to leave their cars on the street. Parking was $10 or $24 for valet. Certainly helped keep the drink prices down.

A black town car pulled up and Aiko put the new couple into the backseat. He watched the car drive off before he used a keypad to open an unmarked door. His shoulders slumped and he sighed as the door clicked shut behind him.

"Slipping up to your apartment alone again?" asked Cleo.

Aiko started and spun around. Cleo was sitting on the floor, leaned against the door leading to Outrageous Fortune drinking horchata from the taco place down the street.

"Didn't mean to startle you," said Cleo.

"Just tired," said Aiko. "Maybe I'm coming down with something."

Cleo shook his head. Aiko could see the gray roots Cleo worked so hard to hide.

"You haven't been sick a day in the last thirty years," said Cleo quietly.

Aiko stared at his manager. Cleo had been with him since the day Aiko had staggered out of Lafayette Park. Two lonely youths against the world.

Cleo had aged. Aiko had not.

Cleo pressed his back against the door and slid to a standing position set his drink aside and wiped hands on his pants.

"Has it been that long?" asked Aiko. He knew it had.

Cleo looked at him sadly. "I still don't understand you."

Aiko kissed Cleo's cheek. "You don't have to."

"Someday you're going to send me away like all the rest."

Aiko shook his head. "I can't." Cleo desired only one thing: to stay at Aiko's side. To be whatever Aiko needed him to be.

Cleo grabbed Aiko's slim wrist. "You don't have to be alone."

Aiko pulled away. "I have earned my penance."

Aiko passed through two security doors, up the key carded elevator, entered a code and fingerprint to unlock his penthouse apartment. When he pulled it open there was an arrow stuck into the back of the door directly at eye level. When Aiko's fingers brushed against the silvery arrow it disintegrated to lead dust and the carnival ticket pinned beneath it twisted slowly to the ground.

He ran to the open window, embers of hope glowing once more—but there was no one there. Agony ripped sound from his throat and tightened his hands to talons.

Aiko tore the clothes from his body; fingernails and straps leaving marks on his skin as he pulled fabric apart. He flung himself on to the bed and screamed into the mattress until he couldn't breathe. He raised his head to gasp air, sobbing breaths slowing until misery and pain gave way to sleep.

Aiko awoke in darkness. The sheets were twisted around him and moist with sweat. He strained to feel to the edges of his extended perception.

The carnival was here.

He pulled on pants and grabbed his things. It had rained while he slept. The cement was rough and damp beneath his bare feet. He was half-way to the park before he realized the carnival ticket was clutched in his hand. He didn't remember picking it up. He crumpled it into his pocket and picked up his already frantic pace.

Dark energy swirled around him, rushing past as the carnies set up in Lafayette Park.

Stop. Go back.

But he couldn't. Tears streamed over his cheeks as he winged towards the park. Thirty years. Aiko could feel the ticket pulsing in his pocket. Pulling him home.

He sped through the park, down twisting paths. Faint music and laughter floated on the wind like fragments of a nightmare. Memories of a life long gone. The leather strap across his chest chafed, his skin unused to its presence. The weight between his shoulder blades felt strange after so long without it.

His feet alighted on the iron gate of the heroes' cemetery, the statue of Lafayette silhouetted against the city's lights. The bronze statue stood with a coat draped over one arm, the other outstretched, fingers splayed in offering. Aiko glided to the statue and placed his hand in its cold, stone grip.

"Time in the world has turned you crazy," said a mocking voice. "Running around in the dark, shaking hands with statues."

Aiko jumped to the statue's shoulder and peered into the darkness.

A figure in white leather balanced atop a tall obelisk monument. "It is time to stop running, brother."

"No." Aiko reached behind his back, fingers pinched around the fletching of an arrow.

The black-haired reflection of Aiko sighed. "Don't do this."

Aiko's voice came out in a whine. "You know what I did, Anteros. What I did to you."

"The balance is upset. Do you have any idea what it's been like with you gone? Vengeance with no forgiveness, Absence without reunion?" A dark bow spread out of Anteros' left hand and he notched an arrow into it.

Aiko reached behind his back and in a flash of light produced a shimmering arrow. A golden bow spread from his other hand. "Brother, we don't have to do this. Let me go."

"I will never let you go. The carnival will never let us go." Anteros' arrow flew through the air and struck Aiko in the leg.

The arrow sliced through Aiko's pants but the instant it touched his skin it burst into dust.

Aiko fired.

The golden arrow hissed harmlessly past Anteros' right shoulder.

Anteros watched it pass. "I will finish what you started, brother." He dove.

A leather-clad shoulder connected with Aiko's chest, knocking him off the statue and they both slammed into the side of a mausoleum. Anteros recovered first. He dissipated his bow, circled around Aiko, shrugging one arm then the other out of his jacket, discarding it and his quiver on the ground.

"Fight me with your own face, brother."

"This is my face now," whispered Aiko. "My avatar."

"You have forced it and your punishment upon me as well," said Anteros gliding closer to Aiko. "You stole your face from a man who wanted death"

"I gave him his heart's desire," said Aiko.

"No more running, Eros." Anteros reached out and touched Aiko's bare chest. "We belong to the carnival, brother, and I will bring you back."

At Anteros' touch, they both changed. Wings ripped from their flesh, limbs shortened and swelled with baby fat. Their bodies became those of small children, but the features were still recognizable as Aiko's. The cherub that had been Aiko—now Eros—flexed and spread his wings, feather tips brushing against his back.

"That's better," said Anteros, his voice high and childlike. He reflected Eros except for long dark hair and butterfly wings of shadow and crimson.

Eros lunged for his brother and their bodies struck mid-air. Eros shoved one end of his bow under Anteros' chin and flipped him backwards. He used his wings to follow his brother's arc through the air, grabbed a handful of black hair and whip-cracked him into a tombstone. Anteros slid against the marble and hit the rain-softened ground with a thud.

Eros folded his wings and dove feet-first into Anteros' back. Anteros rolled away at the last second. Butterfly wings brushed against Eros's toes as both cherubs spun in opposite directions. Anteros' chubby hand managed to snag the quiver on Eros's back and pulled his brother to the ground.

Anteros scrambled over Eros, stomped a foot into the back of his neck and drove the golden-haired cherub's face into the mud. The dark-haired cherub climbed to the shoulders of a stone angel and took flight. As he flew away, he fully extended both sets of wings. The dappled crimson of his butterfly hind-wings looked like splatters of blood.

Eros wiped the mud from his eyes, shook out his feathered wings and leapt into the air. The smell of fried dough and popcorn wafted on energy-thickened night. He twitched a wing and soared upwards on a thermal. The carnival was being set up all around him in the park. Trucks of parts and pieces were parked along the wide asphalt paths. Many hands raised tents while dark magic constructed the timber bones of the roller coaster around him.

He could hear them now. The inhabitants of the carnival below. He could feel their desires, long unfulfilled.

Something had happened to the carnival. It had never been friendly, but there had been a wild cacophony of gleeful chaos, not the seething maelstrom of destruction that roiled beneath him now. He swooped low to inspect the heart of a stilt-walker from the Danse Macabre and found it locked beneath an iron-coating thicker than the deepest grief.

Eros willed his bow into being and shot an arrow into the stilt-walker's heart. The golden arrow sparked against the iron, but could not crack it. He fired another and another. His arrows didn't even leave a scratch.

"You see? It only grows worse every day you're gone." Anteros swooped through the air above him. "We finish it now, brother. One way or another."

Anteros held a glimmering apple.

Every night since he'd left the carnival, Eros had dreamed of the apple. Of his own small hands wrapped around its golden weight as he'd placed it on his brother's head. Looking down a dark arrow shaft, his fingers releasing before he woke up in a sweat, heart dull in his chest.

"Anteros!" There were tears streaming down Eros's face as he shot towards his brother.

13

The Ferris wheel came to life between the brothers, lights pulsing and calliope music ever-swelling without crescendo. It shifted uneasily, steel complaining as the empty seats gently swayed and the malevolent wheel spun ever on.

Anteros darted between the spokes of the Ferris wheel, cocked back his arm and flung the golden apple back towards Eros. The apple seemed to lazily spin through the air on a high arching path towards Eros until the instant he twitched wings to move out of its way. The apple screamed like a tabernacle choir of cats in heat and the world began to deviate.

The Ferris wheel split in half becoming a giant maw of metallic spoke teeth. The teeth snapped at the flying cherub, metal groaned and clanked. Eros folded his wings and streaked towards the ground with the screaming apple following at his heels like a heat-seeking missile.

He shot straight through the game booths; balloons popped, metal bottles clanked and giant stuffed animals tumbled in his wake. Nothing slowed the apple behind him.

Eros threaded the carousel animals and grabbed the brass ring off the pole as he blew past. He barrel rolled and threw the ring at the apple.

It dodged.

"Shi-" Eros never got the chance to finish.

The golden apple overtook him. Its considerable weight and eerily accurate aim sent him into darkness.

Eros awoke with his hands and feet bound to the wheel of Sateen, the Razor Dancer. His quiver was missing. There was something heavy affixed to the top of his head—the apple.

"Welcome ladies and gentlemen of Le Carnaval Pomme D'or, cast your eyes upon the vile creature tied to the wheel."

The unseen voice was the ringmaster's, evoking the man's red turban and waxed mustache in the cherub's memory. Eros thrashed, trying to see as much of the tent around him as he could. Carnies populated the grandstands. He could see the

14

Malvolo twins in the front row, black sequined vests sparkled in contrast to dull hate-worn eyes. The swirling gossamer robes of the woman known as the 8th wonder of the world caught Eros's attention in the audience as she leaned forward over Sateen's shoulder to get a better look at the bound cherub. Sateen's eyes locked on Eros's across the circus ring and she smiled—the rows of silver needle-sharp teeth promised otherworldly torment.

He turned away. A hand wrapped in Eros's hair and jerked him forward. Anteros looked sadly at his brother. He made a chubby toddler fist and punched Eros in the jaw.

"Thirty years." There were tears in Anteros' brown eyes. "You selfish coward."

Eros tasted blood. "Kill me." The words sounded slurred.

"Why should you get release?" Anteros' cherubic lips sneered. "Deserter."

"We have rules?" asked someone in the audience.

"Sure," said another, "rules that there are no rules."

Unkind laughter filled the tent.

Anteros pulled a golden arrow from Eros's quiver. "Released from your hand, I can't touch these without destroying them." He tapped Eros on the nose with the flat of the arrowhead.

"It was a joke," sobbed Eros. "I couldn't hit the apple on your head, the arrows just went around."

Anteros shoved his chest in Eros's face. "Does THIS look like a joke?" A scar marred the left side of Anteros' chest.

Eros flailed against his bindings. "I don't know how one of your arrows got in my quiver!"

"That arrow hit more than one heart," said Anteros touching Eros's chest. He stepped back from the wheel. His dark bow stretched into being.

The apple seemed to get exponentially heavier. Eros strained to keep his head upright.

Anteros notched the arrow and pulled the bow back impossibly far. He sighted but didn't fire.

Anteros' arms shook from holding the draw. "What is your desire, Eros?"

The string twanged and the arrow pierced Eros's chest. All the loneliness and longing he hadn't felt for thirty years burst under pressure from his heart. Liquid fire filled his heart, melting the iron cage around it. Molten metal dripped and burned trails down his soul. All the pain from a purpose unfulfilled, tried to tear him apart. There was a breath, then the pain began anew— only this time it was Anteros' pain, made worse by the knowledge that it was his fault.

Eros screamed. His voice gave out after a few minutes but air still expelled from his lungs. With each rush of pain a little more iron dripped off his heart.

Hours, days, or minutes passed. Eros had no way of knowing. He struggled to regain his breath, his awareness of mind. His heart thumped unhindered in his chest and his head felt lighter. The golden apple lay at his feet; his tears glittered like dew on its metallic skin.

Eros closed his eyes. He could feel the glow of desire still trapped behind iron in those around him. The carnival still seethed with vengeance, but he could sense cracks in the iron around their hearts.

Tiny hands released him from the wheel and Eros collapsed onto his brother's shoulder unable to even twitch a wing under his own power.

"Welcome back," Anteros whispered in his ear.

There was so much work to be done.

Minerva Zimmerman lives in a secret lair in Oregon where she trains spiders as minions. She spends her days trying to avoid being killed by history and her nights plotting world domination. She has no outstanding warrants, but has had trouble renting demolition equipment since the events in Ontario. For more of her work check out Growing Dread: Biopunk Visions

Funhouse
Erik Scott de Bie

The day Stardust took his kids to Le Carnaval Pomme D'or—the Golden Apple Carnival—was a beautiful day. Dark grey clouds embraced the horizon at dawn, but the sun burned them away to nothing, leaving cheery blue in their wake. A warm breeze caressed the gleaming grass. Jets buzzed in the sky, leaving smiling trails of cloud.

Nothing could go wrong on this day. It was a perfect day.

"What could go wrong, Beth?" Jaccob Stevens asked as he loaded the ice chest into the car. The kids chased each other around him. "It's a perfect day."

"Yay!" the kids said together.

Elizabeth Stevens wore that patient, long-suffering look that only the wife of a popular and public super-hero who runs a multi-billion dollar corporation can quite muster.

"I agree, honey," she said through a tight jaw. "It's a perfect day. Just perfect!"

Her words didn't match her expression, however. Her mouth held menace, and her eyes a sort of mourning as if she couldn't bear to see him go. Jaccob felt a little funny about that, but it was only a momentary hesitation.

"Let's go to the carnival!" Jaccob said in that enthusiastic way of his.

"Yay!" said the kids.

The carnival encamped in the south end of Lafayette Park filled Cobalt City with lilting music, drawing children from their beds like mice dancing to the tune of a mystic piper. Cries of the amazed and laughter of the amused rose to greet them as Jaccob ushered the kids through the front gate.

Strange. With the stories Jaccob had heard of the carnival, he figured that it operated only at night. This place didn't seem dark or creepy at all, but bright, clean fun. It filled him with bliss.

"Where do you want to go first, kids?" Jaccob asked.

"Everywhere, Dad!" said Michael. Charlotte was staring with eyes big as moons.

They approached the front kiosk of the carnival, which was attended by a two-headed man who looked half-human, half-hippopotamus. A bright gold nametag adorned his shirt, marking him as Chris Chimera. "Welcome to the Golden Apple Carnival, Le Carnaval Pomme D'or!" said one of Chris's heads. The other head gave them all a sly wink. "Kids ride free today."

"Yay!" said the kids, and immediately disappeared amongst the rides, the popcorn stands, and the multicolored tents.

Jaccob almost wished he was wearing his Stardust armor, just so he could keep track of them on the personnel radar. But the carnival overwhelmed him with a feeling of such blissful serenity that he didn't really see the need. Of course nothing would happen to them.

Why would it? It was a perfect day.

The various attractions caught his eye, each of them named with letters sculpted in sparkling multicolored lights. The sword-swallowing Malvolo brother, clad in gold chainmail and adorned in a green cloak like the Errol Flynn Robin Hood, amused a horde of cherubic children by sliding long swords from a quiver on his back and plunging them down his throat, while his fire-breathing twin brother lounged in the shadows. Kitarra the Cat Lady bounded about her sphere-shaped cage, pouncing upon mechanical mice and offering the men who watched her appreciatively a series of snarls. Face wrapped in shadow despite the spotlight that followed him everywhere he moved, Questo the Mentalist directed volunteers from the audience with only the power of his voice. Jaccob watched as they fell to the floor as though held down by an awesome weight they could not see.

Somewhere deep in his gut, Jaccob felt uneasy. Maybe it had to do with Beth, back at the house—the way her words hadn't matched the look she gave him. Something felt wrong.

"Oh!" Stardust exclaimed. He fumbled a flashdrive out of his pocket, where it had been digging into his leg. "That explains it."

It was a Starcom Industries drive, adorned with the corporate logo. He'd never seen this flashdrive before, and wondered what it might contain. Not that he had a computer—the carnival was decidedly low-tech, and he hadn't seen the need for his armor.

"How did you get there?" he asked the flashdrive.

He looked up and saw a woman watching him from the shadows of the big top tent. She stood beneath a rough-painted sign that said "Staff Only." Unlike the crowds of people laughing and smiling, this woman wore a blank expression and looked at Jaccob directly, as though they were having a conversation from across the intervening distance. She had eyes of livid white and a timeless face that defied the easy application of age.

He waved, but she gave no acknowledgement. He couldn't imagine she was blind if she was staring at him so intently. Many a super-villain had stared at him in much the same eerie way, and on those occasions, it had been far less creepy.

Jaccob was just about to start over there when the kids returned. "Daddy, Daddy!" said Mike. "There's a show in the big tent, with lions, and tigers, and bears, and—"

"Oh my!" said Charlotte. "Can we go? Can we? *Can we?*"

Jaccob looked up to where the mysterious woman had been standing, but all he could see was a swaying tent flap where she must have gone inside.

"Sure, kids," he said, burying the unease that had passed over him. "Let's go see."

"Yay!" said the kids.

The flashdrive seemed to have disappeared at the same time. Jaccob forgot all about it.

The show truly was remarkable, with death-defying trapeze artists, lion tamers as big as three men, and a whole parade of clowns that seemed to explode into showers of multicolored confetti. Mike and Charlotte whooped or exclaimed in delight as beautiful women pirouetted through the air and a spangled woman hurled knives at her handsome assistants leaning against targets. The obscenely tall, turban-topped ringmaster announced each act in sequence with the sort of grandiose manner that incited ever-louder cheers from the gathered audience. And cheer they did, raising their voices loud enough to strain the canvas roof of the tent against the poles that held it in place.

Through it all, Jaccob felt as uneasy as he had before. Something about this just wasn't right, but he couldn't put his finger on it. The sights and sounds thrilled him, but at the same time, he couldn't focus fully on the show. His eye kept wandering the performers, searching for—there. At the edge of the ring, under the big top, was the woman he'd seen before. She watched him with those weird empty eyes of hers.

"I should put on my armor," he said, though he couldn't credit the idea.

Putting on the armor would spoil the whole show, and it would not be like Cobalt City's most fabulous super-hero (his agent had cautioned him to use the word "famous," but he liked going old school) to disrupt the fun of paying customers. There was no danger here—just his own creepy feeling about some lady with the crazy eyes. Also, it would be seriously uncool. So instead Jaccob kicked back and did his best to relax.

Then he noticed his kids were missing.

At first, he thought it was just a misperception, as if he hadn't been paying close attention and he was just looking the wrong way. But no, they had definitely been sitting on his left, and now those seats were empty.

Sweat broke out over his face and neck and his hands shook. "Mike? Charlotte?"

Jaccob looked around, his blood suddenly thundering in his head, but he couldn't see them. "Excuse me," he asked his neighbors, "have you seen—?"

The couple sitting beside him looked his direction with slack-jawed faces, their eyes dull and senseless. As he watched, they grinned at him with ridiculous mirth, then turned back to the show and whooped with sounds that were not quite human.

Jaccob clasped his hands, in and out. He felt itchy all over, and sweat made his clothes cling to his skin. He didn't know what to do.

"My armor," he said.

He kept a suit of lightweight armor in the trunk of his car. Maybe he could go get it...

No time, though—not when his kids were missing.

Jaccob shoved through the strangers watching the show and started down the steps, two at a time. A lion tamer was demonstrating his valor by putting his head and various limbs where his vicious charge could easily bite down. The crowd went wild with vicarious victory and he looked up, only to see the man wrestle the great cat to the ground. He thought the faces in the big top looked inhuman, gripped in lust for the show. They seemed more like hazy caricatures than real faces: distorted as though by searing heat.

Dizzy but unsure why, Jaccob managed to catch himself on the edge of a bleacher, only to see the kids—hand-in-hand with the white-eyed woman he'd seen earlier. She was leading them from the big top.

He hurried after them, elbowing his way through groping hands that tried to restrain him. His rough passage drew indignant squeals as of pigs, rather than humans—when he looked, his fellow circus goers looked indeed like wallowing hogs. He felt ill in the pit of his stomach.

What was going *on*?

"Magic," he murmured. "Man, I *hate* magic."

21

He pushed out of the big top into the night, which felt agonizingly cold compared to the sweltering closeness inside. When had the sun set? Surely they hadn't been watching the show *that* long. Jaccob shivered in his short-sleeved shirt and missed his armor's climate-control function. That, and target scanning, so that he could track the woman through the dark carnival.

Night transformed the place into something out of nightmare. The twinkling, multi-colored lights became, as the moon rose, smoldering torches that oozed greasy smoke. The names of the various carnival acts remained, spelled out in tangled wires of electric lights the color of blood, but seeing them stopped Jaccob short and made it hard to breathe.

No longer did Malvolo swallow swords, but rather arrows—arrows fired at him by a pair of pudgy cherubs while impish children watched all around him. He was trying to dodge them, but over and over they struck and his cloak and chainmail swallowed them up. And his face…

"Huntsman?" Jaccob stammered. "My God!"

Sure enough, Marcus Castille—the Huntsman and his fellow hero—was trapped in the circus game: the subject of a shooting gallery for those winged creatures with their bows. Blood ran from his mouth and his eyes pleaded for aid.

Jaccob looked back in the direction he'd been running: he could still see the woman leading Michael and Charlotte, not moving too fast. He could help and still catch them. Jaccob stepped toward them, and the creatures turned their bows on him. He raised his hand to deflect the missiles, but realized his bare hand had no such power. He didn't have his armor—he was powerless.

Instead, he turned and ran, arrows whizzing around his head. The Huntsman's cries of pain followed him as he ran. "I'm sorry," he said. "I can't!"

He had to keep following the woman who'd taken his children. She was moving around the Cat Lady stand, grasping a child by either hand.

"Mike! Charlotte!" he cried out. "Wait!"

Inside the cage, a feline-like female cried out in terror as she tried to get away from dark-skinned men that had joined her in the spherical cage. They looked like demons, with eyes that glittered with flame and impossibly wide smiles on their faces— smiles that dripped blood down their cheeks. Worst of all, Jaccob realized their quarry was not Kitarra the Cat Lady but his furry friend and colleague Wild Kat. Everywhere she turned or leaped, she cut herself on the cage, which seemed made of razor wire.

She locked eyes with him and gave him a desperate mewl, but what could he do against demons? He had no armor.

"I'm so sorry!" he cried, and ran on.

At the mesmerist's stand he had seen earlier, Questo was gone, and instead Dr. Shadow hung spot-lighted in his place, suspended in the air as though nailed by magic upon an invisible cross. At first, Jaccob could not see his friend's tormentors, but then the shadows moved and he could make them out: dark silhouettes rather than men, which raked their incorporeal claws down Dr. Shadow's body. Where they touched, the claws drew lines of black blood that seeped down the sorcerer's limbs in rivulets.

Again, Jaccob's heart felt as though it would break, but he could do nothing to help. Without his armor…Jaccob Stevens was just a man with mortal hands, which could do nothing against creatures without physical bodies.

He wondered if every member of the Protectorate was here, in one form or another, being tortured by the Golden Apple Carnival. He wondered if he would see all of them, and not be able to help any of them.

"Daddy?" asked Charlotte's voice, carrying across the dark carnival grounds. He saw them again, in the distance, at the door of a building with mirrors attached to the front like windows. The funhouse.

He could do nothing to for his friends, but maybe he could save his children.

Jaccob left Dr. Shadow to his fate and ran on, hating himself for every step.

The funhouse loomed, a crude structure of iron sheeting grown rusted with years of neglect. The mirror-windows cast back distorted images of himself and the surrounding carnival. He could see twisted versions of the death traps in which his fellow heroes languished. He couldn't think about that—he had to save his children, armor or no armor. He plunged through the doors.

A long hallway stretched deep into the funhouse, every inch of which was hung with mirrors of every shape but rectangular. As he stepped inside, his image raced down both sides of the hall, the reflection picked up by a thousand looking glasses. The mirrors stood at slightly different angles, so he saw only splintered reflections of himself—part of his face here, an arm there, and so on. The composite that he saw was a gaunt wreck of a man, crushed by grief, panic, and helplessness into something less than a man. He thought he looked less human than those demon creatures he'd seen torturing his friends.

"Daddy?" asked Charlotte, just as Michael asked, "Dad, where are you?"

Their voices echoed down the hall, defying Jaccob's efforts to place them. He turned back toward the entrance, and realized the hall of mirrors stretched back as far as he could see forward. He must have wandered in without realizing it, and now he was lost among the mirrors.

The white-eyed woman appeared in the mirror, next to his reflection, and he whirled, fists raised. Maybe he had no armor or powers, but he'd thrown enough bare-knuckle punches to be familiar with the concept. The ageless woman stared at him wordlessly.

"Where are my children?" he demanded. "Give me back my children!"

She said nothing, but only stared at him in absolute silence. He couldn't say if her expression was triumphant or sad.

"I'm warning you!" he said, starting forward.

The woman started to turn, and Jaccob caught her shoulder roughly. Or, at least, he would have, except that his hand struck a mirror that promptly shattered. Razor-sharp glass cut into his hand and blood welled in its wake. In his state, with adrenaline saturating his body, Jaccob felt it no more than he would have had he worn his Stardust armor.

"Cute," he said, picking glass out of his cut hand. "But I've seen *Enter the Dragon* too, lady. Now bring me back my—"

His words trailed off when he saw himself in a mirror across the hall. He might have expected to look bloody, strung-out, and horrified, the way he had when he'd passed through the doors of the funhouse, but the image before him was Stardust: Jaccob Stevens in his armor.

"Huh," he said.

The likeness was perfect and mirrored his movements exactly. Its hand rose to match his when he looked at it, wondering whether he'd have armor on. He didn't. The reflection was smiling, its face partly hidden in Stardust's mask. Jaccob couldn't shake the feeling that he was laughing at him—at himself.

He opened his mouth and the reflection did likewise. When words came, however, they were not his—instead, the reflection spoke without him.

"Don't worry, citizen," Stardust said. "I'm here now. You're safe."

Jaccob blinked. "Yeah, but—what?"

The Stardust in the mirror flexed his arms and grinned wider. "Cobalt City doesn't need Jaccob Stevens on this one," he said. "It needs me—Stardust."

"But—but I'm Stardust," he said.

"You're Jaccob Stevens," the reflection said. "A pathetic weakling of a man whose only saving grace is that he occasionally puts on a suit of extra-terrestrially-powered armor and becomes me." He put his hands on his hips. "A hero."

Jaccob looked around, and all the mirrors near him showed similar images: armored champions with the wide shoulders and narrow waist of the classic hero, standing in poses of strength and skill. They all wore armor of some type, some loud and bristling with devices, some slick and streamlined like fighter jets—some bright with clashing colors, some metallic and black for stealth. Many were blue and gold similar to his Stardust armor, and he realized he might be seeing different possible versions of himself—alternate Stardusts from other worlds and other stories.

"See?" said the reflection behind him. "We're all here to save the day—and not one of us failed to dress for the job. Well…" The voice seemed to speak right into his ear. "Except you."

Jaccob turned and caught his breath. The nearest Stardust loomed over him from out of the mirror, gauntlets burning with the power of his armor mingled with a dark sort of fire.

Even as he cringed into a helpless ball on the floor, Jaccob felt something cutting into his thigh. He fumbled in his pocket and pulled out the Starcom flashdrive he'd found earlier. At that moment, just before he was about to die, he looked upon it like a message in a bottle, one he wished he could read.

A message from himself.

"Wait," Jaccob said, holding up his empty hand.

He hadn't really expected that to do anything, but sure enough, the reflection stopped in mid-loom. It regarded him quizzically.

"This isn't right," he said. "This isn't me."

"You're right," said the reflection. "I am Stardust. You are nothing. We don't need—"

"No, no, I heard that part—it's very trick or treat kind of scary," Jaccob said. "But what I mean is—this thing here, this isn't right. This isn't really happening."

The reflection may have been a demonic version of Cobalt City's most popular hero, but it quirked its eyebrow in a way that was very Jaccob Stevens pondering a new chemical formula. "How do you mean?" he asked.

"You really had me going," Jaccob said. "A perfect day turned into a nightmare, kids lost into a carnival of terror, my friends being ripped apart by insane carnies. But you messed up."

"Oh?" said the reflection, either genuinely interested or humoring him.

"When I was outside," Jaccob continued. "I saw my friends—Huntsman, Wild Kat, Doctor Shadow—being murdered and I just ran." As he spoke, mirrors around him shimmered into those awful images, and he saw himself break down and flee in helpless horror.

"What's so surprising about that?" asked the reflection. "You are helpless without your armor. A coward. A worthless worm—"

"Right," Jaccob said. "See the thing is—and my wife gives me grief about this all the time—when I see someone in trouble, I can't *not* help. Even if I'm hopelessly overmatched, I throw myself into it headlong."

"And fail utterly," the reflection said. "You'd sacrifice your children for the sake of heroism? You are a bigger fool than—"

"No, you still don't get it," Jaccob said. "I could have helped. For instance…" He looked at the mirror with the Huntsman, being shot by his own arrows. "I'm a multi-billionaire, owner of a preeminent tech company, and one of Cobalt City's premier super-heroes. You don't think I could have thrown in for some aikido lessons?"

Abruptly, the image in Huntsman's mirror changed, and Jaccob saw himself wading through the impish archers and audience, hurling the creatures this way and that, blocking arrows with demonic children's bodies, and shattering limbs with punches.

"And Kat," he said. "You think I would have just left her like that, when a little casual application of simple electricity would make all the difference?"

The image of Wild Kat's cage shifted, and he saw himself shouting an instruction to jump as he tore free one of the moldering wood posts of the carnival grounds, bringing with it sparking cables of blood-red electric lights. She leaped just before he touched the cables to the spherical cage, and the creatures within jerked and cried out, electrocuted.

"And I may not know the first thing about magic," Jaccob continued, "but even I know Doctor Shadow does better outside the light."

In the mirror, Jaccob picked up a brick and hurled it into the spotlight that shone upon Dr. Shadow. The radiance instantly died, and the sorcerer plucked himself from the clutches of his enemies and did his magic thing. The demons screamed.

"And my kids," he said. "Them, you did the worst."

An image appeared of Michael and Charlotte stand at either side of the white-eyed woman. Their eyes were wide and vacant, and they looked terrified.

"First of all, Mike and Charlotte never agree on *anything*," he said. "Certainly not which rides to go on and which shows to see, much less wandering off hand-in-hand with a perfect stranger."

The image shifted again, and abruptly the kids were pulling at either of the woman's hands, trying to draw her in two directions at once. The serene witch-woman looked confused and more than a little nervous.

"And," Jaccob said. "Again, I'm a multi-billionaire, owner of a preeminent tech company, and one of Cobalt City's premier super-heroes. You don't think I would have invested in protection for my own children?"

Abruptly, armor unfolded out of Michael and Charlotte's belts, cloaking them in protective gear that struck back at the woman kidnapping them. She fell, dashed to the ground by a shockwave of sound from Michael's gauntlet. Then, when she reached out for balance, she touched Charlotte's armor, which sent a pulse of electricity down her arm and knocked her senseless.

"And if they're not real," he said to Stardust, "then none of this is real."

"So what's your point, Jaccob Stevens?" asked Stardust in the mirror. "All these things you could have done, and yet you did nothing. You children are better warriors than you. You lack the strength and confidence if you don't have me. Without me, you are nothing."

"That's *exactly* my point," Jaccob said. "Here—in this place, or dream, or whatever it is—without you, I'm nothing. I'm not brave, or strong, or smart, because that's the way you set this up. And while the rest of the Protectorate may think I snored my way through Dr. Shadow's lectures about trapping spells, I remember two things: one, you can't attack me directly. And two, if you're going to mess with your subject's free will, you leave an opening—a weakness."

"An opening?" said the image of Stardust. "And what is that?"

"You," Jaccob said. "Specifically, you telling me exactly what I needed."

Then he slammed his fist into the mirror. Pain bloomed in his hand and cracks spread along the glass. Seven years' bad luck, he thought.

"You're the focus of all of this," Jaccob said. "You're the worst part of me, and you are seriously in need of a swift kick in the butt."

He could hear it now—a woman's voice droning in the background, filtering through the broken mirror. This was it. This was right.

"Stop," said Stardust. "You'll hurt yourself. You can't—"

Jaccob didn't listen. He struck again, bloodying the other hand, then again, and again.

"Stop, you fool!" Stardust backed away in the world of the mirror. His hands gleamed with the energy of his gauntlets. "I'm warning you—"

Jaccob looked at the flashdrive in his hand, balled up his fist around it, and struck one last time. The mirror shattered, and all around him—all down the hall—mirrors shattered in a storm of glass shards that cut unprotected flesh to hamburger.

Unprotected flesh—unlike his. Down his arms and over his hands, he wore glistening blue armor. His torso glowed with starlight and his boots crunched on the glass underfoot.

The hero was back.

Jaccob Stevens was back.

"Now," he said as the dream fell apart. "About that swift kick in the butt…"

Awareness returned to Stardust slowly, swimming in the milky depths of the hypnotist's blind eyes. Then suddenly he was himself and he gasped, choking on smoky air like boiling fog.

He sat in the hypnotist's tent, across a small table from the woman he had seen in his dream with her white eyes and ageless face. He looked down and realized their hands were clasped so tightly that bone-white flesh spread around his fingers and hers like creeping frost in the sweltering tent. Her empty gaze held him prisoner as much as her hands.

Stardust clutched her hands tighter to keep her from pulling away, and his teeth gritted as they wrestled. She was a tiny woman—more bone than muscle—but she held on with the strength of a locked vice. Their hands began to shake.

He would get out of here, round up the rest of the Protector, get his armor…

"Dad?" asked a sleepy voice.

Perched on the stool beside him, Michael rubbed his eyes and yawned. Charlotte was there too, leaning against Stardust—Jaccob—and snoozing.

"Dad, I'm tired," Michael said. "Can we go home now?"

He looked back to the hypnotist, and saw red capillaries bloomed around her dull pupils. Was she smiling?

"Yeah," he said.

He eased his grip, and the blind lady did so as well. Her sightless gaze remained upon him, asking a question without words.

"Mike, Charlotte," he said. "Let's go."

When Stardust let go, the hypnotist released him with the slightest hesitation. He thought she gave him a tiny nod, but he might have imagined it.

Jaccob took his sleepy daughter in one arm and held Michael's hand. The boy smiled up at him, and the world seemed a little lighter.

As he left the tent, Jaccob could swear the blind white eyes followed him.

Erik Scott de Bie writes speculative fiction from under an abandoned military compound in Seattle. He takes inspiration from music, movies, and his cats, who form the basis of his genetic experiments. (So far, all that kibble has only produced bigger cats, but he's holding out for more exciting results.)

Primarily a fantasy author, he has published four Forgotten Realms novels: *Ghostwalker, Depths of Madness, Downshadow*, and the forthcoming *Shadowbane* (due out this fall). His work has also appeared in numerous anthologies such as *Beauty Has Her Way, When the Hero Comes Home*, and *Cobalt City Timeslip* from Timid Pirate Publishing.

If his work delights, frustrates, or perhaps just entertains, hunt down Erik on facebook or twitter (under his full name), or at his website (www.erikscottdebie.com), and give him your feedback.

Harrigan the Magnificent
Matt Adams

Curls of smoke swirled within the casino.

"Hit me," Harrigan said, clutching a stiff drink in his right hand and waving the thick smoke away with his left.

"Dealer has Blackjack."

As luck would have it, Harrigan would have none.

He gave the table a gentle tap with his fist and got up.

If he'd wanted, he could've read the dealer's mind and taken the House for all its worth.

Not that the House at Cobalt City's dingy C.C. Money Casino had much to give up. Business charlatans ran the place. Gambling charlatans flocked to it. The casino didn't have much to win, a truth those who hit the jackpot found out the hard way. Serious Quayside gamblers threw down their cards at the Forbidden Palace.

Harrigan learned his lesson there a long time ago.

The House always wins, especially when you cheat.

He walked toward the exit as a world-weary casino girl strutted past in a vain effort to catch his eye.

He gave the girl a fake smile.

She returned it.

With that, Harrigan downed the last drops of his drink and handed her the glass.

He put his shoulder into the casino's mucky glass door and left without looking back.

Trickles of sweat eased down his forehead.

Cobalt City in the late summer. Shoulda checked the weather.

He almost always wore a tan trench coat providing him with a modicum of cover. Just a day before, the night air was crisp and a hefty wind came off the water.

An increase in humidity gave Cobalt City an oppressive feel and Harrigan struggled to breathe the thick air. Had it been daylight, he would've seen the tell-tale streaks of sunlight bouncing off the streets in a mirage of constant movement.

As was often the case in New England, the weather changed its mind. Someone, it seemed, had flipped a switch, transforming cool nights into sweat-it-out affairs. He thought about the air conditioner back in his apartment and tried to remember if he'd paid his electric bill.

He probably had; Cobalt City Power and Light hadn't sent a disconnect notice yet.

Harrigan gazed across the river at the bridge leading to the Cannonade. A dim, colorful glow emanating from the side of a building caught his eye.

A series of posters covered the dark brick, plastered one over another in an endless sea of advertising excess.

Le Carnaval Pomme D'or.

Harrigan didn't know the phrase, but he didn't have to. On the poster, a glowing, golden orb floated above a series of candy-striped tents. Small portraits at the bottom seemed to float.

Then, the pictures *moved*.

A man who looked like a fish.

A woman whose smile revealed fox-like features.

A puffy-shirted rapscallion who appeared to toss a sword from hand to hand while his apparent twin swallowed flame.

Harrigan shook his head to clear it.

The pictures were static.

Must be losing it.

According to the poster, the carnival would arrive in Cobalt City tomorrow.

An unsettling feeling crept into Harrigan's stomach. He turned to look at the Cobalt City Tech Shoppe billboard erected on a sunken hill near the bridge entrance. The bright, blue letters no longer announced discounts from the city's electronics store.

Now, a golden orb floated above a circus tent. A woman faded into the picture, her face made up like an ancient Egyptian. Strands of dark hair flowed down her shoulders, glimmering like an oil slick.

A wide smile formed on the woman's full, crimson lips.

She pointed at Harrigan and the words on the billboard changed to read, "Join us tomorrow."

Harrigan turned back toward the posters.

Instead of a sea of individual fliers, the woman now took over the whole wall. Up close, he caught the intoxicating smell of an exotic perfume.

The words changed again: "Join us tomorrow."

Harrigan backed away.

The fliers disappeared, replaced by dark, red brick.

He turned.

The Cobalt City Tech Shoppe sign advertised a buyback deal for smartphones.

A voice in his head.

"Join us tomorrow."

"Ladies and gentlemen, I welcome you to Le Carnaval Pomme D'or!" a tall ringmaster announced. He wore a black suit and red turban. "To the uncultured among us, that's the Golden Apple Circus."

The crowd cheered.

Harrigan didn't join in.

A certain insidiousness belied the sweet smell of cotton candy and the salty scents of peanuts and popcorn. The families of Cobalt City didn't feel it; they gobbled up their snacks and slurped their sodas in anticipation of an entertaining afternoon.

"I guarantee you an unforgettable show, ladies and gentlemen. You will experience a once-in-a-lifetime thrill!" the ringmaster said with a wide, sweeping bow.

Again, the crowd cheered.

Again, Harrigan refused to join.

"And now for our final act of the evening, I present to you the amazing, the incredible, the mind-blowing beauty of the Enchanting Elena."

Harrigan froze in his seat as the raven-haired beauty glided toward the center of the coliseum.

The ringmaster offered her his microphone, but she waved him aside.

"I am the Enchanting Elena," she announced. Her voice boomed through all corners of the venue without the aid of the microphone. "It is my pleasure to entertain you this evening."

The woman stopped and smiled at the breathless gasps from the crowd.

Most came from men.

This time, Harrigan joined in.

"I have abilities some only dream of," the woman said. Her voice carried a foreign accent, but Harrigan couldn't place it. "I can lift anything with a thought."

She looked at the ringmaster, who now floated several feet in the air.

The man let out a confident laugh as the audience gasped. He landed with a flourish and spread his arms while bowing to the woman and backing out of the spotlight.

"I can turn the entire audience into puppets," Enchanting Elena said. "I want everyone to raise their right hand."

The right arm of every audience member shot up into the air except for Harrigan's.

The woman's eyes narrowed and Harrigan heard a voice in his head.

I said everyone.

The intrusion into his mind angered him, but Harrigan complied.

"Very good," the woman said. Her hand traced from her neck to her waist. "Very good. You may put your hands down."

"Now that you have seen what I can do, I require a volunteer," the woman said.

Dozens of hands went up. Scores of men and women shouted for the Enchanting Elena to pick them.

The woman cleared her throat. "A young volunteer, please."

The hands of dozens of disappointed men snapped to their sides.

Harrigan felt the presence in his mind again. Even from far away, he could see deep into her dark eyes. They stalked him with every move he made, every breath, every shift in his seat.

The Enchanting Elena looked over the crowd and picked a little boy in a yellow-striped shirt who sat a few rows in front of Harrigan.

The spotlight turned on the little boy, who made his way down the aisle as two attendants walked him to the woman.

She whispered something into the boy's ear and he smiled.

"I have shown you my mastery over the art of persuasion," Enchanting Elena said. "Now I shall make this little boy disappear!"

The crowd whooped and hollered as the woman rubbed her hands together. She put her fingers up to her temples.

"Your name is Nicholas, yes?" the woman asked.

The little boy in the yellow-striped shirt nodded.

"I understand, Nicholas, your favorite movie is *Cars*," the woman said.

The little boy gave an emphatic nod.

The Enchanting Elena smiled and patted his head, "Do you see my power?"

The audience laughed.

Harrigan did not.

"Now I shall make little Nicholas disappear," she said.

She clapped her hands, creating a bright cascade of brilliant, yellow-white light.

36

When the light disappeared, Nicholas was gone.

The crowd cheered.

Harrigan pressed a hand up to his forehead, *Where did you put him?*

The answer came as a whisper in the woman's exotic voice.

He is gone, Harrigan. Yes, I know who you are.

With that, the show ended.

Harrigan exited the red-striped tent with the rest of the crowd, following Nicholas' parents closely. Like the other members of the audience, the boy's parents laughed and cheered after their son disappeared.

Harrigan shuddered from an uncomfortable chill and pulled his coat tighter. He kept close to the boy's parents, waiting for someone from the carnival to reunite them with their son. Instead, the couple continued walking through Lafayette Park.

Harrigan stretched out with his thoughts.

Neither parent seemed concerned.

The boy's father pulled open the driver's side door and Harrigan slammed it shut with a thought. The startled man looked up.

"Must've caught the breeze," Harrigan said.

The man said nothing about the stillness of the afternoon.

"I guess so," he replied.

"Did you enjoy the show?" Harrigan asked.

The couple exchanged confused looks.

"It was quite a show," the wife said.

"What did you think about the final act?"

"Amazing. Simply amazing," the man said. A glazed look overtook his eyes.

"Your son. Aren't you going to pick up your son?"

"I think you have us confused with someone else," the woman said, her tone pleasant but halting.

"The kid who disappeared at the end…isn't that your boy?" Harrigan asked.

"Sir, you're making us uncomfortable," the woman said.

Harrigan took several steps toward the couple and held out his right hand.

The man's wallet flew from his back pocket to Harrigan.

He rifled through it to find a picture of the couple with the boy who'd disappeared at the circus.

The husband held up his hands, "Please, take whatever you want. Just don't hurt us."

Harrigan rolled his eyes, "I'm not going to hurt you. I want you to look at this picture. Who's the boy?"

The man took a step back as Harrigan's large frame lumbered toward him. Harrigan put the picture on the hood of the black SUV and backed away.

"Just look at the picture. Tell me who the boy is," he said.

The man and woman quivered as they came around to the front of the vehicle.

"I don't see a boy in this picture," the man said.

The woman let out an exasperated sigh. "It's just us. Like it's always been."

"What do you mean 'it's just us'?" Harrigan asked. His right hand shot from his side and the picture leapt to it as if on an invisible string.

In the picture, the couple smiled. They were in the same pose, except the boy was no longer there.

Harrigan shook his head, "I'm sorry, folks. I must have you confused with someone else."

He returned the picture and stood with his hands on his hips as the shaken couple climbed into their vehicle. The SUV almost backed into another vehicle before stopping abruptly and peeling away. Harrigan closed his eyes and returned to the moment just before the boy disappeared. He saw the couple pat the child on the back before the boy bounded down the steps to meet the two attendants.

Now, they had no memory of their little Nicholas.

He retreated Quayside to the familiar confines of the C.C. Money Casino.

The usual dealer at his favorite table had the night off, but Harrigan took a seat anyway. He needed to think, needed a place to clear his head. He waved away the casino girl who brought him a comp drink.

Gotta keep my head clear. Don't need that. Not right now.

"Change," Harrigan told the dealer, who accepted his dog-eared twenty-dollar bill with admirable grace.

The dealer laid out the cards, showing her seven to Harrigan's eighteen.

"Stand," he told the dealer. It was the wise play, the safe bet.

The dealer nodded and turned up a king.

She'll have to take another card. Odds in my favor.

Harrigan's smile faded as the woman pulled out an improbable four of clubs.

Of course.

"Dealer has Blackjack," the woman said.

"Yeah, yeah," Harrigan sighed.

"Another hand, sir?" the dealer asked.

Harrigan shook his head, thanked the woman, and walked away.

His mind quickly turned from his latest Blackjack setback to the missing little boy and the parents who no longer remembered their only child.

Words echoed in his head, *I know who you are.*

He needed answers.

And he needed them before Le Carnaval Pomme D'or left Cobalt City. Only one person came to mind.

Grey.

In Karlsburg, small shops crammed themselves into the strangest nooks and crannies, a concession to years of taming the rocky, shifting terrain. The narrow, zigzagging roads twisted and split off into wild directions. Those who didn't know where they were going could end up miles away from their destination just by following the wrong branch of a street.

According to the fliers, the Main Event still had seven shows remaining: one on Friday and three each on Saturday and Sunday.

Harrigan had until Sunday night to find the boy in the yellow-striped shirt. The name "Nicholas" stood at his memory's edge. A few seconds ago, he had forgotten it. Focused concentration brought it back. He knew the Enchanting Elena was behind the mind intrusion.

Harrigan walked through the disjointed streets of Karlsburg, the atmosphere atypically dead for Friday night.

He leaned against a light pole and tapped it three times, repeating the act seconds later.

His eyes found the moon, which was just now beginning to show. A slight but discernible wind churned up in the dead evening before an ashen mist appeared in the cloudless sky.

To his right, the ashen cloud solidified, forming feet, then legs, then a torso, arms, and a head. With an unsettling *whoosh*, clothes materialized, including boots, a long coat, vest, tie, and wide-brimmed hat.

"Nice of you to drop by," Harrigan said.

The formless man reached up to adjust equally formless ashen-leather goggles. "It is good to see you tonight, dear boy. And why have you summoned me this evening?"

The cultured, British tone of Mister Grey.

"The circus is in town—"

"A carnival, actually," Mister Grey corrected. "There is a subtle difference between the two. The circus by definition—"

Harrigan held up a hand, "I don't need the etymological differences between the words."

Mister Grey's head jerked back slightly and tilted.

"That's right. I know a few big words," Harrigan grunted. "I wanted to talk to you about the carnival palm door."

Mister Grey laughed. "I'm certain you mean Le Carnaval Pomme D'or."

"However you pronounce it," Harrigan said. "My Italian is a little rusty."

"But the term is"

"I'm pulling your leg, Grey. Metaphysically, of course."

Mister Grey straightened. "I see. What troubles you tonight?"

"I went to the show this afternoon and a woman called the Enchanting Elena made a little boy disappear."

"That must have been a spectacle."

"Trust me, Grey, it was. But the boy who disappeared isn't around anymore. His parents don't even remember him."

Ash floated from Mister Grey's arm, forming a cane for him to lean on.

"The parents don't remember their child?"

"That's right. I followed them to their car—"

"That must have been quite a scare for them," Mister Grey interrupted.

Harrigan pressed on, "And they couldn't remember having a child. I took the man's wallet and found a picture of the couple with their son. When they looked at it, they didn't see the boy. When I looked at it again, the picture just showed the parents. It's as if the boy never existed."

"Are you certain this isn't a mix-up?" the ashen hero asked.

"See for yourself."

With that, Mister Grey dissipated into a cloud of thick ash. Harrigan started to cough, but Mister Grey's non-corporeal self flooded into his nose and mouth.

Seconds later, the hero emerged and reformed as Harrigan tried to contain a coughing fit.

Mister Grey stood with both hands balanced on his elegant ash cane. "There has been an intrusion into your mind, Harrigan. An intrusion to all who witnessed the event. Those

41

who aren't trained in the telepathic arts will never know what happened. Whoever this Enchanting Elena is, she's quite powerful."

Mister Grey shifted on his feet. "Something like this happens each time Le Carnaval Pomme D'or comes to our fair city. They pose as entertainers and lovers of family entertainment. I fear by the time they finish their run here, more will disappear."

"Any ideas on what to do next?" Harrigan asked.

A slight breeze blew through Karlsburg and Mister Grey briefly dissolved.

"I would call on Doctor Shadow," he said.

Harrigan snorted. "We don't get along very well."

Mister Grey let out a droll chuckle. "I had forgotten. I can put in a good word for you."

"It won't help," Harrigan said. He shook his head, "He still thinks I botched the operation down in the Hollows."

"You'll go it alone, I take it?"

"I always go it alone."

He sat down at a small table inside the Cobalt Crab, a low-key, Mom-and-Pop operation where the staff knew him well.

Stephanie brought him his usual order, the Crab Punch, a Long Island Iced Tea with a little extra kick. He took a sip and spat out blood, realizing Stephanie was no longer Stephanie.

The Enchanting Elena stood before him now, her long, black hair almost blue in the bar's dim lighting.

No one else noticed her.

Harrigan tried calling for help as the woman sat down, but his throat felt too tight.

"Harrigan, you pathetic fool," she admonished. The words flowed both from her mouth and head, "You would've been wise to ignore my invitation. You would've been wise not to come to the carnival."

The invisible rope around his throat loosened, "What are you talking about, lady? You practically begged me to show up. That was you on the sign. Don't deny it, you wanted me—"

The invisible rope tightened and Harrigan spoke no more. The woman placed her smooth fingers on his chapped lips.

"You are one of the lesser ones here," she said in her exotic accent.

It could've been Scandinavian.

Maybe Romanian.

Harrigan couldn't tell, but he certainly didn't like being considered "lesser."

"But you are much more than you appear to the others," she soothed as she ran a hand over his right shoulder. "You have abilities no one realizes. Except maybe Doctor Shadow."

The invisible noose grew even tighter before Harrigan closed his eyes and made it go away. He sprang forward in his chair and pushed into the woman, knocking the table over and ending up on top of her.

Closer now, her perfume filled his senses, overwhelming Harrigan to the point where his head spun. The woman closed her eyes and spasmed in apparent rapture.

"Yes. The power of the mind. I feel it inside me," she said. "You can use this to get whatever you want, yet you abuse your power by helping others."

Her hand shot to the back of Harrigan's head and she pulled him closer, pressing impossibly soft lips against his own.

Harrigan closed his eyes and drank her in for several uncontrolled seconds before regaining his senses.

He opened his eyes to find the Enchanting Elena gone, replaced by a terrified Stephanie.

The interior of the Cobalt Crab spun, its dingy neon lights and tall barstools swirling as strong hands picked him up. Before Harrigan could say another word, he was skidding across cobblestones.

Mick the bartender-slash-bouncer shouted something about never coming back.

Harrigan got to his feet and swore.

Of course it's raining.

Harrigan awoke with a headache unlike any other before. His dreams were strange, even tortuous.

He felt the Enchanting Elena's presence in his mind throughout the night. His strongest mental shields could not keep her out. Only through intense concentration had he kept her from overtaking him as she had at the bar.

The newspaper told Harrigan it was Sunday, a fact he found surprising considering he'd returned to his apartment late Friday night. Whatever the enchantress had done to him, she'd made sure he didn't interfere with her work at the carnival.

He rubbed his forehead and tried to remember when Le Carnaval Pomme D'or planned to leave town.

One show Friday, three shows Saturday, three shows Sunday.

He could still make it to the carnival's final show. Harrigan wondered who had disappeared during the performances he'd slept through. No doubt six families were missing children they didn't even know they had, thanks to the Enchanting Elena.

Harrigan sent a psychic pulse out to Mister Grey.

He didn't need help, but he did have an idea.

"I would prefer to do this in the safety of the Keep or my haunt in Karlsburg," Mister Grey said. "I don't care much for the Hollows."

Harrigan grunted. "The rent is cheap, Grey. If you haven't noticed, this hero stuff doesn't pay much."

"I find the spiritual rewards quite satisfying."

"You're a floating dust bunny who doesn't have to worry about rent," Harrigan said.

"If it is your intention to insult me, Harrigan, then I shall leave."

Harrigan held up his hands in an effort to calm down his friend.

"It's a joke. I asked you to come here because I have some questions for you. This girl, the one from the carnival, she keeps talking like I'm someone special. She keeps saying she 'knows who I am.' You have any idea what that means?"

Mister Grey emulated pacing by floating back and forth with his chin tucked within a ghostly hand.

"To my knowledge, there is little extraordinary about you, Harrigan. Born in Ohio to normal parents as Miles Almont Harrigan. Powers did not manifest until college. As a dropout you sought the training of Doctor Shadow and moved to Cobalt City. Your, ahem, partnership did not work out, leaving your abilities considerably powerful but rather raw. You've spent time as a security guard, a barfly, a luckless gambler, a rogue, and a quasi-hero. It is a boring story as far as this city goes."

"Thanks for the encouragement, Grey," Harrigan said. "It makes me wonder why this woman insists on bothering me."

"Perhaps she's attracted to a penniless antihero?" the specter mused.

Harrigan uncorked a powerful punch at Mister Grey's torso, but his hand passed right through the phantasm.

"You're not much fun, ash-face," Harrigan said. "But you have some mind powers of your own. What have you felt from the carnival?"

"You mean the carnival palm door?" Mister Grey asked, recalling Harrigan's earlier verbal gaffe.

Harrigan crossed his arms.

Grey continued, "I have been around for a long time, my brutish friend. Three decades ago, this very same carnival came to town. Their enchantress used a different name back then. Her act involved making young children in the audience disappear."

Harrigan reached for the ghost's lapels, but again his hands passed right through.

"So this has happened before?"

45

Mister Grey tipped his hat, "Bravo."

"How did you defeat them last time?"

"Defeat is not the word I would use," the ghost said. "I would employ 'survived.' That's what they did thirty-odd years ago. They survived. Malevolence lurks amongst the rides and games and sideshows. It is a nearly unstoppable darkness that calls from the deep."

"I have to stop her," Harrigan said. "What she's doing isn't right."

"You would be best to head to the Keep and convince others to help you," Mister Grey said. "But I'm sure they've already planned something. Perhaps going it alone would surprise her."

Mister Grey touched Harrigan's head with wavy hands.

Harrigan felt the intrusion, although it didn't feel like the violation the Enchanting Elena had brought upon him. Certain portions of his mind closed down and others opened up.

Mister Grey shot backward and floated in mid-air.

"I have fortified your mental defenses, Harrigan. She will not be able to detect your presence until it is too late."

With that, Mister Grey dissolved into millions of tiny particles and drifted away, leaving Harrigan to wonder what magic potential the living specter had unlocked within him.

Harrigan ran toward Lafayette Park wishing he'd hailed a taxi. As he rounded a corner, he caught his reflection in the shining glass of the Cobalt City Toy Emporium and stopped.

His mirrored image wore neither a trench coat nor dark shoes.

He also appeared several inches shorter than his 6'5" frame.

He now dressed in bright colors: a lime green, striped shirt with outlandish orange shorts and tennis shoes that lit up with every step.

He looked down at his own body to see he still wore his tan coat, light armor, and shiny black shoes.

Another glance up at his reflection confirmed his resemblance to 12-year-old Miles Almont Harrigan, horn-rimmed glasses and all.

Must've been some work Mister Grey did on me.

Harrigan continued until he made it to the carnival's entrance.

The sign read, *"Kids 12 and under get in free."*

Finally. Some luck.

The tall ringmaster delivered his usual spiel, followed by the requisite elephant and flying trapeze acts, a strongman, a clown car, a sword-swallower, and more.

The finale still awaited.

"Now ladies and gentlemen, children of all ages, you will experience a once-in-a-lifetime thrill! Welcome the Enchanting Elena!"

The woman simply *appeared* next to the ringmaster.

This time, her dark, flowing hair had been braided, twin snakes curling up either shoulder.

The Enchanting Elena went through her routine, levitating the ringmaster and forcing the audience members to raise their hands.

"Now that you have seen what I can do, I require a volunteer," she said.

Hundreds of hands shot up, many accompanied by the screams of men and children excited by the possibility of meeting the enchantress face to face.

Harrigan stood on his seat and jumped in hopes of attracting her attention.

The Enchanting Elena pointed directly at him.

It worked!

Harrigan bounded down the narrow steps past a few aisle vendors hocking popcorn and cotton candy. Two attendants met him at the entrance to the carnival's main area.

He stood face to face with the woman, who delivered a genuine smile.

"And who do we have here?" she asked. Her arms swung out wide in exaggerated bravado. She placed her fingers on her temples. "And your name is…" She paused and looked confused, as if reaching for something she couldn't quite get. "What is your name, precious child?"

"I'm Miles," Harrigan said. "I'm pleased to meet you."

The crowd roared at his response and the enchantress waited until the ruckus died down.

Again, the Enchanting Elena strained to pluck something from his mind. "What is your favorite movie, dear Miles?"

Dammit. Movie. Think of a movie.

"I like *Cars*," Harrigan said.

The woman wrinkled her nose, "Hmm. Yes. That seems to be a popular choice among the boys."

The audience laughed at her delivery.

"For my next trick, I shall make young Miles disappear," the Enchanting Elena said. Small beads of sweat dotted her forehead.

She clapped her hands together, creating a vortex of swirling, yellow-white light.

It hit Harrigan with the force of a runaway semi, but he held his ground and pushed it back at her.

The crowd gasped and then broke out in raucous cheers.

The vortex widened even more, expanding until the top edge touched the inside of the big-top tent at its apex. Harrigan heard voices.

Get me out of here!

I want my mommy!

When can I go home?

Please someone help me!

He shook his head, "Feeding on the souls of children!? Is this what the Enchanting Elena prides herself on?"

48

A panicked murmur rose from the audience. "It's okay, folks! This is all part of the show!" the ringmaster said.

Harrigan sensed relief sweep over the crowd. The murmur subsided.

The woman took several stilted steps forward as the vortex grew and swirled even harder, generating gale-force gusts that pushed Harrigan away.

"You're no child!" the enchantress said. She struggled to gain her footing. The vortex had the opposite effect on her, pulling her braided hair toward it. Her feet dragged across the ground in the direction of the opening.

A name flashed in Harrigan's memory.

Nicholas.

"Nicholas! Get outta there! Come here! Bring your friends!" Harrigan yelled.

"I can't!" a plaintive voice yelled. "She won't let us go."

Harrigan hunkered down and took a halting step toward the opening.

And another.

And another.

Slowly but surely he approached the rift, struggling as much to reach it as the Enchanting Elena struggled to keep away. He didn't know how much time passed before he finally stood before the vortex's opening.

He held out his hand and a small hand took it.

He pulled out a boy in a yellow-striped shirt.

Nicholas.

A burst of energy drew the Enchanting Elena even closer.

"There are more of us," the boy said.

"Eight, right? One for each show?" Harrigan asked.

"There's a lot more than that, mister," Nicholas said.

Harrigan sensed both amusement and confusion from the crowd. The ringmaster's showy proclamations seemed to have the desired effect.

With each child pulled to safety, the vortex drew the Enchanting Elena ever closer. Before long, children filled the entire floor underneath the big-top. The Enchanting Elena now stood a foot away from the opening. After making sure the children were safe, Harrigan approached her.

"What you have done is despicable!" he yelled, struggling to hear himself over the whipping winds of the rift. "Using kids to power yourself! Erasing the memories of entire families! How did you live with yourself?"

The woman's hair remained as dark and foreboding as before, but lines ravaged her once-smooth face.

She grabbed Harrigan around the waist and kissed him; this time her lips were sandpaper.

"Thank you," she whispered as she flew into the yellow-white rift.

Seconds later, a small girl—Harridan didn't think she could be any older than ten—took a tentative step out of the rift and joined the other kids.

Like the Enchanting Elena, her hair looked dark as midnight.

The vortex no longer tried to push Harrigan away. Instead, it drew him perilously closer. He strained to remain standing and several of the kids grabbed him in order to prevent him from going in.

They were all being pulled into the rift again.

"Let me go," he said. "I understand."

With that, the tiny hands binding Harrigan to the corporeal world let go.

He flew into the rift, which closed to thunderous applause.

Matt Adams is a TV news producer whose short stories have appeared in Wily Writers for Speculative Fiction, A Thousand Faces, and anthologies from Library of the Living Dead Press. He lives and works in Indianapolis, Indiana, with his wife and (possibly) man-eating frog. You can check out more of his work at http://mattadamsauthor.blogspot.com and find him on Twitter @statomatty.

Custody Battle
Charlie Kenmore

He could feel the pressure building even through the dense clouds. Dawn approached. It was almost time. It would be painful, but it was the only way. Besides, physical pain was nothing besides the psychic pain of his repeated failures to save her.

It had taken him centuries to figure it out. His body bore several scars from previous failures. All of the auguries suggested that this is where they would make camp. He had to be in place when they arrived. Otherwise, once the tents were up, their combined wards tuned to his unique metaphysical footprint would keep him out, yet again.

He took the matching jet-black amulets out of his pocket, then shrugged off his hooded black cloak with its scarab medallion, leaving himself naked and exposed to the elements. He folded the cloak and placed it on top of the package resting by his feet. It took over forty years and tens of thousands of dollars just to find all of the ingredients. It took another thirty years to craft the amulets, refining, recalibrating and retuning the vibrations until they were in perfect synchronization. It took another thirty years to pour enough power into the amulets to hold the spell in place for at least thirty days, having only an approximate arrival date.

Standing naked in the cold pre-dawn mist, he placed one amulet in each hand, and closed his eyes. The timing was critical. He had to invoke the spell at the exact moment that was neither night nor day. The cloud cover made no difference. He did not have to watch for the sun. The countdown was based on the pressure building behind his eyes. Three. Two. One. In a tongue so old he doubted it was human in origin, he whispered,

"Schi^iich^aagakha." A line of fire sliced through his center, pulling him apart in perfect bilateral symmetry. But like a single cell undergoing cytokinesis, his entire body duplicated itself, replacing the missing halves, until two identical Dr. Shadows stood side by side. They turned to each other, and said simultaneously, "Hello, handsome."

The closer Dr. Shadow reached down and picked up the folded cloak and the package beneath it. He handed the cloak with the scarab clasp to his identical twin, then opened the package and removed two sets of clothes, including two dark tunics, another black hooded cloak, and the golden sash and sigil inscribed medallion that he always wore in public. The newly formed twins dressed. Each secreted his amulet in an inside pocket. The one who would remain put on the sash and the medallion.

The fully adorned Dr. Shadow closed his eyes, took a deep unnecessary breath, and slowly sank into the ground. The remaining Dr. Shadow carefully policed the area making sure there was no visible trace left of their presence. Satisfied that the area was clean, he lifted off the ground for the short flight back to Regency Heights. "See you soon."

It had been twenty-three days. Dr. Shadow had not turned on a light or left the house in all that time. Of course, without the medallion, he was loath to go out in public. That fact notwithstanding, since the split, the photosensitivity that normally only bothered him outside in the sun, now burned in the glare of a forty watt bulb.

Every couple of nights, he ordered some unwanted carry-out dinner or an unnecessary sundry from the local pharmacy for delivery after sunset. He always accepted and signed for these items personally. That way, the carnival's spies and scryers could report that he was still at home.

He pulled the amulet from his pocket, and held it up to the sputtering taper candle that provided all of the light for the room. The amulet was a bluish-gray. It was lasting a little better than expected. But if it was not used in the very near future, it could be another century before he could try again.

The barker watched the two men approach. The Carnival opened at sunset. The early crowds were thinner than he had hoped. But considering the drizzle and cold, it was not bad for mid-week. It took the barker all of five seconds to work up a complete profile on both of them: early twenties, unmarried and unattached (possibly still virgins—at least the one on the right in the faded Metallica tee shirt), college educated, first full time jobs. They would do nicely for starters.

"You there. Stop pretending not to look, and come on over. This is your only chance to view the Eighth Wonder of the Ancient World, the Enchantress of Alexandria, the timeless mistress of beauty, Iboni. As she has down through the ages, she will mystify and mesmerize you, tease and tantalize you." The barker's voice dropped to a stage whisper, "And give you the woodies of your life." He raised his voice, "Only five tickets."

The possible virgin in the Metallica shirt gawked at the life sized posters on either side of the tent flap. His buddy poked him in the back. "You know what they say, don't you? When you stare into her breasts, her breasts stare back."

"Huh?"

"Never mind. Let's go."

"No, I want to go in." The PV reached into his pocket and pulled out a string of tickets that he bought at the front gate. "You coming?"

"Naw. I'm going to head over to the midway. I'll meet you by the Ferris wheel at 9:00."

Dr. Shadow rose silently up through the ground. He released the stale breath that he held for the last twenty-nine days. He found himself behind a trailer, out of public view. Still, he knew that he was being watched. He started toward the front of the trailer, but stopped short with the first low warning growl.

His encyclopedic memory immediately identified the species, and his acute hearing pinpointed source. There was no point to turning invisible. This species did not hunt by sight. There was no point to sinking back into the ground, even if he had time to spare, which he did not. The creature would only wait for him to reappear, whether it took a minute, a day, a month or a year. The growl belonged to a Lilith's Hell Hound. Once locked onto prey, the hound would hunt until its prey was dead. Period. End of discussion.

Lilith's Hell Hounds were virtually impervious to harm. One could shoot them, stab them, or burn them, and then watch the wounds heal while the hound bit off your arm (which Dr. Shadow knew all too well from experience—a spasm in his painfully and laboriously regrown right triceps accompanying the thought). They felt no pain. The two principal methods for fighting a Lilith's Hell Hound were to stand still and let it kill you quickly, or kill yourself before the hound had a chance to bite your face off. Fortunately, experience had taught him a third method.

The sense of wrongness that surrounds a Lilith's Hell Hound preceded its appearance in front of him. Dr. Shadow braced himself. His reaction had to be instinctual and reflexive, rather than conscious and deliberate. The beast was too damn fast.

He concentrated on the medallion hanging on his chest. Five of the sigils glowed. As his eyes registered a black and tan streak headed his way, a portal opened half a meter in front of the medallion. The streak flashed into the portal and disappeared. The portal immediately closed.

He had no idea where he had sent the hound, and would have to be extra diligent the next time he stepped through a portal.

He made his way to the fence, and stopped a meter from the edge of the darkest corner of the carnival grounds. He reached out, *I'm here*. A shadow crossed in front of him. Seconds later, his twin landed a meter away on the other side of the fence. They held up the opaque milky white amulets. They shook their heads. Another day or two would have been too late. Without a word, the twins undressed.

The twin on the outside placed the amulet between his right thumb and index finger and extended it toward fence. The inside twin held his amulet between his left thumb and index finger, and extended it forward until the two amulets touched. On contact, the two amulets flowed together, disappearing as the twins drew closer together. As their index fingers touched, the twins' bodies connected. Both twins used their indomitable forces of will to clamp their mouths shut to hold in screams from the molten agony coursing through them.

Their arms were almost subsumed. Now came the really tricky part. As their shoulders touched, the inside twin braced his feet and leaned back away from the fence. The outside twin leaned forward, and threw his weight toward the fence. The combined effort shifted the majority of their mass a mere micron or two inside of the perimeter, but it was enough. They continued to conjoin inside the carnival grounds. After a minute of blinding white pain, a single Dr. Shadow stood naked in the cold drizzle. He took a moment to center himself, then dressed and headed toward the lights.

Most people gave the old man a fairly wide berth as he swayed from side to side, staggering and slowly lurching toward the Ferris wheel. Obviously, the man had had too much to drink. Regardless, most people would tend to avoid making contact with an octogenarian wearing a Metallica tee shirt.

Dr. Shadow felt the confusion and despair emanating in waves from the old man. He sensed there was a disconnect between the man's current appearance, and his natural state of being. Although it pained him, tonight the old man would have to be collateral damage. He continued past the old man towards the sideshows. He paused for a moment and watched the couples bickering as they exited the Tunnel of Love. Honestly, what did they expect at the Carnaval Pomme D'or? As he passed the shadow of a large oak, he turned invisible.

The barker froze. The marks remained all in place. But something was amiss. A rat poked its nose out from under the left hand corner of the tent. He considered throwing something at it, but had nothing at hand except the ticket box. He settled for a low snarl, "Of course I sensed it. But I can handle the front. I don't need your help. You go check the back." As the rat disappeared back under the tent, Dr. Shadow slipped in through the front entrance.

He paused, tasting the air with his tongue (a talent learned centuries ago as an acolyte of Set). It would take years to list all of the scents and tastes, but they all fell into several distinct categories: lust, fear, anger and despair. He focused on the strongest category, lust, and isolated a rich pungent pheromone masked by the cloying scent of long extinct Abyssinian Gray Lotus. She was here! His pulsed quickened, but he resisted the urge to run to her. There was still one more test to run.

He focused on fear. It was well hidden, but he knew what to look for. He was disappointed, but not surprised, to find it. He tasted the dark veiled evil that hid under the other scents, waiting to announce its presence once a victim was too enthralled to resist. He knew it of old. He had once been its victim, but surprisingly he survived. Her mother was here somewhere as well.

The tent appeared to be no more than ten meters squared from the outside. But he had been walking for at least ten minutes since entering the tent. He saw the glow shimmering on the tent fabric three meters ahead, and slowed. He tasted the air again. It was heavy with Abyssinian Gray Lotus.

He moved the flap aside, and stepped into the room. A large round wicker basket sat in the middle of the room. Large fluffy throw pillows were stacked around the walls. There were no other furnishing. She stood naked in the basket, her back to the door. Her flawless skin was ebony, a stark contrast to the almost translucent white of his own. Her straight, thick, black hair (inherited obviously from his side of the family) hung down to her tailbone. Her back was swayed, and her firm buttocks were pear-shaped. She was six feet tall, a good half foot taller than he was.

"Hello, Iboni. I am your father. I have come to take you home."

The rat scurried back to the front. The barker shook his head. The rat nodded, satisfied that everything was fine. The barker was not as certain. He placed the "Intermission" sign on the tent entrance and walked over to see whether there were any vacancies at the tattooed lady exhibit.

Iboni swayed gently back and forth. The scent of Abyssinian Gray Lotus surrounded her in a cloud. "Hello, Father. What makes you think that I am not at home?"

Dr. Shadow felt the change in pressure. The medallion stopped the dagger a centimeter from his right eye. He reached up and took the suspended dagger down, turning in the direction of the dagger's path, as a new voice hissed, "And what makes you think for a moment that I would let you take her?"

"Hello, Lilith. I thought I smelled your stench when I walked in. I had no intention of asking for your permission. I merely made an unassailable statement of fact. I have come to take Iboni home."

Iboni turned around. Her breasts were firm and round, and slightly smaller than her frame suggested from the rear. Her stomach was hard and flat. Not surprisingly, she was clean shaven as was the current fashion. All of these things he would have

57

noted, had he been able to tear himself away from her eyes, her terrible golden slit eyes, her mother's eyes.

"So, Daddy, what do you think of your little girl?"

Dr. Shadow did not reply. He knew that the time and energy expended responding would only detract from microseconds he had to raise the shields necessary to save his life. He opted to raise his psychic shields just in time to block Lilith's first mental blasts. His wide peripheral vision caught a shimmer. He knew that Lilith had changed forms. The medallion deflected a blow from her serpentine tail, but the force was still sufficient to knock him two meters to the right and crack two ribs. On the upside, it broke his staring contest with Iboni.

He ducked as Lilith's pointed tail shot by, ripping a meter-wide hole in the tent. He dodged to the left, as the tail ripped through three of the pillows stacked by the wall, leaving a contrail of feathers as it withdrew. He did not like being on the defensive. The pillows gave him an idea. He reached out with his mind and tore open all of the pillows. He called up a whirlwind and filled the room with feathers, blinding Lilith and giving himself time to mount an offensive.

He watched the currents moving the feathers along the far wall and sent a blistering blast of mental energy blast half a meter in front of the tail end. He was rewarded with a scream, and another mental blast hammering against his shields to no avail. He smiled. This blast was only half as strong as the first. Lilith was weakening!

He took a step forward, another blast crackling in his mind. Without warning, Lilith's tail shot around his legs. Before he could react, she looped half a dozen coils around him, pinning his arms to his side. The coils contracted, crushing most of the air from his lungs. Fortunately, he had no need to breathe. The medallion turned white hot as it fought to keep him from learning how a virgin olive felt during its first pressing. Lilith's horrid visage pushed through the cloud of feathers. Venom dripped from her fifty centimeter long fangs. "So, lover. Do you have any last words?"

He nodded affirmatively. He looked her straight in her terrible eyes, and with the last of the air in his lungs, whispered, "Schi^iich^aagakha."

Lilith screamed as a line of white-hot fire seared down the center of her being. The coils crushing Dr. Shadow loosened and fell away as her body began ripping apart. He took a step back and raised a huge ball of searing telekinetic destruction that distorted the air around his temples. "Goodbye, Lilith."

"Daddy, no! Don't kill her! Please, Daddy! No!"

He turned to his daughter, but did not release the energy ball. "I'm listening."

"If you will spare her life, then I will leave the Carnaval Pomme D'or. I will spend one hundred years on my own. Then we three will meet on neutral ground, and I will agree to a joint custodial arrangement. I will spend half of my time with you willingly, and the other half with my mother. But harm her, and I will never see you again. The converse holds true for you, Mother. Harm my father, and I will never speak with you again. Please, Daddy. Do this for me. Do this for yourself. Please, Daddy!"

"And if Lilith will not agree? What then?"

"She will agree. Either way, I will leave the carnival. If she ever wishes to see me again, then she will agree. Mother, hiss if you agree."

Lilith's eyes blazed, but she hissed nonetheless. Dr. Shadow released the energy ball, and the spell of division that was separating Lilith's body. Like a film rolling in reverse, Lilith's body pulled itself back together.

Iboni walked slowly over to her father. For the first time in their lives, they hugged. Iboni laid her head on her father's shoulder and wept quietly. Dr. Shadow put his arms around her and pulled her close, immediately becoming aware of her nakedness. He took off his cloak and wrapped it around her.

"Say goodbye to your mother. It is time to go."

Goodbye, Mother. I will contact you in a hundred years." The hatred in her mother's eyes was palpable, so Iboni added hastily, "I mean it, Mother. Harm him in any way, and we will never speak again."

Lilith took her human form, a form which even Helen of Troy couldn't match. She walked over and hugged her daughter tightly. "Your father will come to no harm by my hand."

"Or your agents, Mother."

Lilith smiled. "You are such a clever little girl. I'm so proud of you. Or my agents. But," she hissed, pausing for effect, "he is never to set foot…no, he is never to place himself corporeally or psychically, or ethereally within the boundaries of the carnival ever again. His presence, in any form, cannot be tolerated. Any violation of this condition terminates this agreement."

Dr. Shadow added one proviso, "Except as may be necessary to ensure Iboni's continued safety, good health and well-being, I will agree to your conditions."

Lilith's slit eyes narrowed even further. "That is unacceptable."

Iboni put her hands on her hips. "Mother!"

Lilith shook her head and offered, "I will agree to brief psychic confirmations of Iboni's continued safety, good health and well-being. But the psychic presence must be limited to that purpose only and must be withdrawn immediately once her status is verified."

"And if Iboni's safety, health or well-being are threatened, I shall have the right and free passage necessary to physically come to her aid."

Lilith paused for several heartbeats, then graciously conceded. "Done. We are in agreement." She hugged Iboni one last time. "Be safe, little one. It is a dangerous world outside. If you ever need me, just whisper my name." She kissed her daughter's forehead, then released her.

"I will be careful, Mother."

Dr. Shadow took his daughter's hand. They walked out of the tent, a trip which took only seconds. As they walked toward the front gate, the tent folded in on itself. The rat popped out just before it disappeared.

Dr. Shadow took Iboni to his home. He introduced the house to her so that it would not attack her if she ever appeared when he was not home. He showed her the bedroom that was hers any time she wanted, leaving the implication open that she need not wait a hundred years.

They shared a simple meal. It was strange to hear another voice in the house, but he found it oddly comforting. Unfortunately, from his perspective, Iboni remained adamant that she was going to spend a hundred years on her own.

Dr. Shadow gave his daughter several parting gifts including new clothes, five thousand dollars and five thousand euros, a summoning ring that could contact him wherever and whenever he was and a farewell kiss. He watched her fade into the shadows. Satisfied that the next hundred years would pass in the blink of an eye, he closed the front door.

Charlie Kenmore is the author of *Earth Angel* and other Seven Realms Tales, several screenplays and numerous short stories. He is a 52 year old professional from St. Louis, Missouri with one very significant other, two grown kids, and two cats. He enjoys collecting books, art and cooking. An avid garage sale hunter, he is still searching for an oil painting by Edouard Leon Cortes (or anything from the Drip and Drool School like Pollack or Rothko that can be sold so he can buy his Cortes). You can find Charlie on Facebook, and at the Seven Realms Earthside Communications Center, http://charliekenmore.blogspot.com/.

Call & Response
Catherine & Andrew Warren

The Carnaval Pomme D'or was on the move again.

Worlds away, they felt it, thrumming in their joint mind(s), singing in their soul/blood, urging them, tempting them unreasonably, tempting them irrationally, tempting them to madness. They knew they must hunt for it, search for it, find it, possess it, consume it. They knew with every drop and gobbet of themselves—knew that IT was there. There, through the worlds, between the sliding mists, behind the closing doors. There, at the carnival, the portal between the pools, a place ill-defended and begging to be pierced.

The carnival was calling them.

IT was calling them…

And they would answer.

"This is not so bad," Ndulu remarked to his older cousin Edirin as they braved the rush of the carnival's main thoroughfare. Edirin wore a suit too nice for the occasion, as usual. From looking at him you might think he was a visiting prince wearing civilian clothes, and you wouldn't be far wrong. In fact, this was Knockabout, one of the most powerful heroes in all of Cobalt City, and one of the chosen heroes of the technologically advanced African kingdom of D'habu.

Dusk was falling over the makeshift streets of the carnival. Flickering tent flaps and threads of sounds, glimmering lights half-seen from the corner of the eye, the peculiar springy feel of sawdust under their feet…Ndulu was happy to have gotten away from the overly sterile-seeming halls of Cobalt City U, and from the rooftop penthouse where the kingdom of D'habu had installed him while he worked towards his degree in Advanced Wave-Particle Equivalency.

And he was especially happy to have ditched those two boring bodyguards who were always following him around. They hadn't been too happy to let him out of their sight, but they could hardly argue with their country's greatest hero when he offered to take Ndulu to the carnival and let them have a night off.

They made him promise to bring his ultra-hyper-advanced gen-beyond-next-gen cell phone, loaded with proprietary D'habu technology, in case he needed to call them for any reason—any reason at all. "Remember! Your knowledge is valuable!" the older one had warned him darkly. Ndulu knew that his kingdom was in talks with StarCom Industries to possibly license some of the cell phone tech for sale in the States, but he hardly thought this would make him, a fairly minor royal relative, any sort of kidnapping target. He was overjoyed to get away from all that and walk down the concourse like any regular American... any regular American in the company of an incredibly powerful super-hero, that is.

Ndulu bit into a dreadful carnival foodstuff: a deep-fat-fried pecan cinnamon roll on a stick, stuffed with coffee ice cream. It had been sold from a grease-spattered stand festooned with the unlikely name of "Cinna-Stick-E-Roll (World's Best)."

"How can you ingest that monstrosity?" Edirin asked in his soft voice.

"It is quite simple, Elder Cousin," Ndulu replied with a respectful twinkle. "One opens one's mouth, quite wide in fact, like so, and..."

Edirin made a complicated gesture that seemed to embody a snort and somehow combine it with an affectionate shoulder punch. The tip of his elbow caught the ribs of a passerby who had drifted a bit too close, and sent the man spinning into two other figures, one robed in scarlet and the other in purple. There was a strange tinkling crash, and...

...the universe slowed down and, at the same time, broke.

Ndulu saw the head of the scarlet figure explode slowly, shards of something reflective spraying out in an arc pattern. He felt the air around them become spongy, somehow; sodden. Squishy.

The scarlet mask slowly fell to the side, revealing the gaping ruins of a face... a face that was hollow. Incongruously, the figure stayed standing, as though its head had not just been caved in; it seemed to still be alive, to be looking at them…

"Get back," Edirin said, his lithe form adopting a defensive pose. Even he, with all his powers, was moving and speaking in slow motion, caught as surely as a mouse in a glue trap. Passersby screamed slowly and stumbled over each other to get away. Edirin remained standing with his weight on the back heel, waiting.

Ndulu's Cinna-Stick-E-Roll sagged towards the ground as he stared at the now-headless scarlet figure. The broken neck jutting out of the robes seemed to be that of a mirrored statue. All around, bits of mirror drifted down, like snow on a windless day.

Knockabout pressed one foot into the earth. Ndulu had seen this move before: he knew his cousin was supercharging gravity to immobilize their strange opponents, and as he slowly crumpled to his knees, he felt the pride swell within. Although he'd watched his cousin many times play-fighting at festivals or exhibitions, and although he'd seen footage of him in action on the nightly news, he'd never before had the chance to witness it firsthand. He saw, in person for the first time, and for the first time he truly felt, that his cousin Edirin was the hero Knockabout.

But although to Ndulu the air seemed almost too heavy to breathe, the mirrored figures were unaffected. They slowly floated closer to Knockable, and the purple one swiveled to face him. Now that he knew what to look for, Ndulu could see that beneath the purple mask and hood, a perfectly featureless mirrored statue was "looking" back at them. Time still seemed slower…slower, and, somehow, moist.

Edirin drew breath—although with nightmarish, painful slowness—and unleashed a sonic boom targeted towards the two figures. Anyone who thought he was soft-spoken would have learned otherwise at that moment; the powerful, deep reverberations actually were a weapon.

Ndulu felt the pride swell within. The power of that sonic blast should have annihilated anything in its path. But the two mirrored statues were unaffected. They "looked" at Knockabout with their empty sockets. The purple one reached up with one mirrored hand to drop its hood. From the back of its head, swirls of pale fluid snaked out. Its masked face remained expressionless as the soft, stringy secretions reached out closer and closer.

Knockabout moved back to get out of range, but it was too slow by half; he wasn't going to make it. Ndulu found himself in a wordless scream as the scarlet one turned to "look" at him with its ruined head. Not knowing what he was doing, he flung his hand out in slow motion…

…and time sped back up. Returned to normal, Knockabout's movements finally took hold and he managed to flip back out of range. Ndulu was speechless, staring at the purple figure. His Cinna-Stick-E-Roll had hit it squarely in the forehead, and had stayed there, incongruously, as the two figures both sagged and then toppled over with twin tinkling crashes, like marionettes with cut strings.

Knockabout breathed out slowly with puffed cheeks, staring at the wreckage before them. Without taking his eyes from the mirrored ruins at their feet, he remarked, "Little Cousin, I believe you have found the one use for that comestible after all."

A surprise, and not a pleasant one; no, my hivelings, not a pleasant one at all, but largely inconsequential. We were parted from IT, parted too soon. IT was there. Within that, and within that one. But it will return to us, we will return to IT, for that is the way of the nine liquids. All things must flow downwards in the end. Especially blood.

"This is not good," Knockabout gravely said. He tucked a Protectorate-issued device back into the breast pocket of his impeccably tailored suit.

"What is not good, Elder Cousin?" Ndulu asked, although he was not certain he wished to know the answer.

"Where the statues stood, traces of disruption remain even now," Knockabout replied. "It as though there are small perforations in the air... in the substance of this world."

"Holes in the fabric of space/time?" Ndulu asked.

"Fabric of space/time? No, that is ridiculous. Where under heaven do you get this idea?" asked Knockabout absently. As Ndulu began to answer, Knockabout cut in with, "We should purchase another of those dreadful American buns. Perhaps it holds the key to repelling more than merely myself."

They made their way back to the food stand near the entrance, only to be greeted with a large sign reading "CLOSED - Sorry for the Inconvenience"

"You must return home," Knockabout commanded. "It is not safe for you here, and you are not trained as I have been, nor has your physical body been imbued with the sacred metal as mine has."

Ndulu knew there was no arguing with his cousin when he took that tone, and so did not even make the attempt. Reluctantly pulling out his cell phone, he punched in a single number...

...and felt his blood freeze and time slowed down and became moist once more.

There were three of them this time: green, yellow, and black, evenly spaced all around them like a triangle of death. The empty mirrored surfaces beneath their masks reflected back the shifting shapes of the carnival. In unison, they lifted their shining mannequin hands to drop their hoods.

From the backs of all three heads, opaque milky-white gobbets of fluid snaked out towards Ndulu. He opened his mouth to scream, but no sound came out; he told his feet to move, but they seemed stuck to the ground. "Caught," he thought, "like a fly in a web!"

Knockabout was likewise caught in the time distortion. Ndulu saw him raise and lower one well-shod foot. A slow-motion blast rippled out, distorting the ground like a tsunami in molten taffy. The yellow and black figures swayed, but stayed upright. But the green figure swayed and toppled, shattering in slow motion as the ground warped under it. Where it had been, bright slashes in the air seemed to hang, as though someone had taken a boxcutter to the air itself.

"That can't be good," Ndulu thought, still struggling to regain control of his artificially slowed body. And he was right. For as he watched, strands of milky white liquid seeped out of those slashes in the air and felt their way towards Knockabout.

The yellow and black figures converged, gliding forward as though they were on well-lubricated wheels. Their blank, reflective heads turned in unison towards Knockabout. And from the backs of their heads, more gobbets of extraplanar sputum reached out towards him.

Ndulu breathed in and began screaming "No!" as the tendrils reached his elder cousin. But by the time he managed to get the word past his teeth, it was too late. Knockabout had been enveloped in tendrils and pulled, whole, through the slashes in the air, along with the yellow and black figures.

Ndulu blinked and blinked again as time sped back up and the air returned to normal. He couldn't believe what he had just witnessed, but there was no way around it. The strange mirrored statues had taken him.

Knockabout was gone.

Ndulu stood still as a statue for minutes after the event. Mindlessly, he put the cell phone back into his pocket. In disbelief, he stumbled towards the spot in the air where the shining slashes had been, but they were gone.

Without his cousin—the hero—to protect him, what chance did he have now? Why were they after him, or them? And most importantly, what could he do about any of it? He had no idea how to contact the Protectorate. Nor did he get the sense that his bodyguard / minders would be able to help…not against a foe like multiple animated mirrored mannequins from another dimension.

Ndulu began walking through the carnival in a daze. Tossed away in a corner he found someone else's Cinna-Stick-E-Roll, and picked it up just in case it actually had some effect against the statues, although he did not think this was likely. More likely that he had merely startled them the first time -- and that then they had returned. But why?

He wandered haphazardly through the carnival. The strange sights and sounds and smells that had at first seemed exotic and diverting now seemed threatening and sinister in the extreme. A clown turning his head slowly—a woman dressed like an eight-armed demon biting into a juicy candy apple—fire-breathers and sword swallowers and jugglers and people hawking trinkets and treats—they all seemed threatening, as though at any moment their masks would be pulled off to reveal the faceless mirrored surface of the hunter statues.

A blue-robed figure suddenly appeared in front of him.

Ndulu jumped back and screamed at the top of his lungs. Only to realize that everyone around him was looking at him strangely. Time had not slowed. The air was not moist.

"Jeez, man! What the eff is your freaking problem!?" the blue-robed figure shouted at him.

"Sorry! Sorry, so sorry," Ndulu stammered, backing away like a stung horse, and stumbled around a corner. He could feel the breath coming quickly and in shudders, and he bent over with his hands on his knees and focused just on breathing. He was afraid, so afraid…

But although he was merely a University student, not trained in the art of combat, he was still a scion of D'habu. Ndulu straightened his spine. He would find a way to outmatch these mirrored statue beasts, and he would do it not with the power of D'habu's mystical metal, but with the power of his mind.

What did he know about them? That they appeared in groups, that they seemed to focus on him and Knockabout for some reason, that they slowed time, that they did not seem to talk, that they inhabited mirrored statues, that destroying one created tears in reality, and that he had startled them away once, so long ago, with a Cinna-Stick-E-Roll.

Grimly, he looked down at the half-eaten roll he'd picked up, studded with dirt and sawdust. "Pah," he exclaimed softly, and threw it to the ground. Buns would be no help to him now.

Looking up, Ndulu caught sight of a billboard outside the carnival. It was lit above and beneath so that it could do its work even at night—such profligacy, Ndulu thought. The billboard blazed with the words: "StarCom Industries - the Future is Here!"

The future wasn't the only thing that was here.

He knew without even looking; he knew by the way time distorted in their presence, a droplet hanging in space eternally, never actually falling...

This time, there were four of them: red, blue, gray, and orange. They appeared suddenly yet slowly, shimmering through the air like visions of water on the highway ahead.

Ndulu had nothing, not even a bun on a stick. He raised his head proudly, knowing that whatever happened, he was an inheritor of the legacy of D'habu, a keeper of its mysteries and a student of its precious secrets.

Suddenly, Ndulu remembered the sacred metal that was the source of his cousin's powers—the metal that was D'habu's most prized possession and its richest hope.

The metal that was currently on the table to license to StarCom Industries.

The metal that existed, in tiny, trace amounts, inside each special gen-beyond-next-gen cell phone produced in D'habu.

Ndulu took the phone from his pocket, slowly—excruciatingly slowly—as the figures closed in on him from four directions.

As the figures drifted towards him with their milky tendrils extended towards his phone, he gave a slow, fierce smile and asked, "Can you hear me now?"

Ndulu pressed the speed-dial button for Knockabout's cell phone.

Multiple tears in reality exploded outwards, scything huge chunks of air apart like meat beneath a cleaver. Time sped up again as the mirrored hunters were sucked through the rents in space/time, which began closing.

Ndulu ran towards the largest tear. Powerful blasts buffeted him as he fought towards the portal between the dimensions. At the last moment, a hand extended through from the other side—a human hand, a hand of flesh and blood—and Ndulu caught it, and pulled, and like a new way of being born, Knockabout reemerged into this world, stumbling and gasping into the dusky, scented air of the carnival.

The tears in the air disappeared. Edirin and Ndulu caught each other in a warrior's embrace after battle, and looked up together at the stars.

The precious liquids were there, my hivelings; IT was there, and we were close; so close. Inside that device, and inside the very body of that creature; we tasted them! We flowed according to the nine liquids towards our goal, but now that channel is closed.

The Carnaval Pomme D'or—that golden apple, taunting us with its smooth skin and juicy tang—oh yes, the carnival is well known to us; well-known indeed, as it should be, for both we and it are drops from the same source.

It seems we have lost this chance at the precious liquid metal of their world. But the carnival will return another time, and when it does, we liquid hunters will return as well!

On the way home, Edirin asked, "What gave you the idea to ring my phone?"

Ndulu was very tired and did not have many words at the moment, but it was his Elder Cousin asking, so he scraped some together.

"I thought they must be after the sacred metal," he said, "and hoped that the same metal, impregnated in your tissues as it has been, would act as an amplifier. Even through dimensions."

Edirin gave a soft exhalation. "Perhaps they are teaching you something useful at this University after all," he commented.

Ndulu was so tired he didn't reply.

His bodyguards had waited up for him. They looked disapproving. While one whisked his outfit away (possibly to be burned), the other asked what on earth had happened at the carnival.

"Well," Ndulu began, his head so light from exhaustion that he seemed to be floating.

"Well," he continued as he lay down, already more than half asleep.

As the bodyguard tucked a blanket over him, Ndulu murmured, "I did run into some chaps with some serious phone envy."

Catherine and Andrew Warren are a husband-wife team in Seattle. Andrew hails from Thousand Oaks, California, and began playing and GMing roleplaying games in the second grade. Catherine is from St. Paul, Minnesota, and entered the gaming world in the 90s. Between the two of them, their interests include cooking, hosting friends, speculative fiction, Latin and Greek, crocheting hyperbolic planes, Chinese, LARPing, higher math, science fiction & fantasy, pickling and fermenting and cheesemaking, shared worldbuilding, puzzles, wordplay, super-hero movies, choral music, Tarot, and a wide variety of other pursuits too eccentric to be mentioned here, including running around after their two charming and high-energy children.

Dance with the Devil
Ashley Bates

My sister and I sat on the dusty blanket, surrounded by the usual crowd noises—the rustling of popcorn boxes, the crackle of a candy wrapper, a sneeze caused by the dust motes floating in the air, a mother's hiss as she shushed her unruly children. The lights under the Big Top dimmed, the footlights went up, and the spotlight shone down upon the figure in the center of the ring.

The trapeze dancer wore all metallic colors, from her gold and bronze leotard to her rippled platinum hair, with a be-jeweled fascinator in her hair and lips that shone like rubies. She kept her kohl-rimmed eyes downcast as she held her opening pose: standing on her right leg with her left leg off the side, toes pointed. Slowly she raised her arms above her head as the trapeze descended from the ceiling. The music piped in over the scratchy speakers grew in volume and complexity as she made a small jump to catch the trapeze bar.

Rising higher in the air, the audience gazed at her flexibility and strength. She dropped one leg and pointed her foot at the floor, while the other leg kept the tension on the rope. Hooking her legs back onto the bar, she pulled herself into a sitting position, and gazed out at the audience waiting with bated breath below her. She took her right-side rope in hand and leaned forward, twisting her torso and reaching out to the audience in a supplicating gesture. The trapeze artist continued with a dizzying display of aerial stunts. Periodically, as she hooked her legs around the ropes and spread her arms wide, or contorted her body around the bar, her eyes closed, as if in prayer.

She twisted and entwined herself in fantastical contortions of body and limbs, rope and bar. With each dramatic fall and graceful movement, the music grew more hypnotic and the audience became more enraptured, unable to tear their eyes away from her.

I know I certainly couldn't.

It was the summer of 1930, the third time that Le Carnaval Pomme D'or had come to Cobalt City, having first arrived in the late 1890's when the travelling carnivals were becoming popular across North America. They pitched tents featuring sideshows, games and thrill acts in Lafayette Park, and our parents had told us about the marvelous experiences they'd had as children on the Midway. The wonders, sights, smells and sounds had created enough fodder for stories for the last several decades.

Now they were taking my sister Tess and I to experience the carnival for ourselves. Tess was 16 and I was 18, and we'd never known such excitement before in our lives. We talked about nothing else for the week leading up to the big event— what games we would play, what sights we would see, what rides we would go on together. It was a tremendous occurrence for me, as I didn't leave the house much: I was crippled from birth, with legs that were crooked and necessitated the use of a wheelchair.

The day finally arrived. We had an early breakfast together and headed out. Other families joined us on the road south of Cobalt City and the excitement was as palpable as the dust kicked up by all of the vehicles that were on the road.

Upon arriving at the carnival and entering through the gate, we smelled the sawdust and sweat from all of the people and the animals. The yells from the hawkers got our attention with things such as, "Come see the freakishly, fantastically two-headed calf!"

Tess grabbed my hand. "Natalie! Look at those posters!" she squealed, pointing with her other hand to placard depicting burlesque woman wearing nothing but sequins and feathers, promising a "titillating experience" for the viewer.

I was more interested in the Amazing Elephant Rider, who appeared to be a leotard-clad beauty on top of the huge gray beast. Having studied the animals of Africa and the Orient in school, I would have loved to see one of the huge lumbering beasts in action.

Mother and Father gave us some spending money, and told us to go and enjoy ourselves. They ambled off, arm in arm, in the direction of the Midway games, joking about who would win the most. Tess and I continued on down towards the sideshow acts and freak shows, with her pushing my chair. The calls of the carnival barkers continued selling their extraordinary features.

"Gaze in wonder at the mermaid from Fiji! Trapped with an enchanted net!"

"Steel and Flame! Watch these wondrous men swallow swords and fire in front of your very eyes! It's the Marvelous Malvolo Brothers!"

"Only a nickel for access to sights from another world! Be the envy of all your friends!"

Each act had its own poster propped out front by the barker, with sun-faded depictions of the act contained therein. While they were certainly fascinating, we passed by most of them, giggling shyly and wondering aloud how such bizarre objects and people were possible. And the combinations! Fish-people and fox-girls, bearded ladies and randy goat-men—Cobalt City might boast a plethora of masked men, mysterious women and immoral villains, some even with amazing powers, but this was something totally different.

We spent hours taking in the sights, mingling with the other fair-goers, taking a break for some cake and lemonade at a stand. As late afternoon approached, one tent caught our eye. The black-and-silver fabric shimmered in the sunlight—or would have shimmered more if it wasn't so dusty—but there seemed to be a slight shadow over the area. It was set slightly apart from the other attractions in the carnival, as if it was a show all on its own.

As we approached, a tall, dapper man with a black moustache approached us, smiling charmingly and wearing a black tuxedo spangled with tiny mirrors on the jacket.

"Good day, young ladies! I am Master Leschone. Are you enjoying the carnival?" he asked, speaking with a slight, unfamiliar accent, a polished clip to his words.

"Oh yes!" we both said. "We've never seen anything like it!"

"You seem like such delightful young women. Are you both from Cobalt City?" the man queried.

I told him that yes, we were from Cobalt City, and how we had been looking forward to the carnival. Tess asked him what event was going on in this particular tent.

"Ah! You are intrigued, are you?" he said with a smile. "Please, you must come in and experience the gravity-defying grace of Kamarina, our trapeze *artiste*. Her performance is unlike anything seen before."

"Ooooh, yes! Let's go, Natalie!" Tess said as she pulled me towards the entrance, pausing only long enough to drop a few coppers into the wooden entry-fee box.

We stepped into the musty, dusty dimness of the tent. Music played softly as we took our seats. Most people sat on large blankets on the ground, with a small ring of chairs around the edges for those unable to sit on the ground, or stand for an entire show. Several minutes later, the lights went out completely, then the footlights turned up, and the dance began. Lighting came from oil lamps placed around the perimeter, adding softly glowing ambience to the show.

As the trapeze artist continued her aerial acrobatics, only occasionally coming back to earth, Tess and I could hardly breathe. I saw Master Leschone tucked back away into the shadows, nodding his head slowly in approval as he watched. When Kamarina completed her performance, she glided towards the dark entryway near the Master. She lifted a black velvet curtain and disappeared as the audience came back to life and dispersed to the rest of the carnival shows. They seemed dazed somehow, walking a bit drunkenly and with vacant eyes.

Master Leschone emerged from his shadowy corner, and was making small talk with a few other audience members. He oozed charm and a bit of oily smugness as he made his way over to Tess and me. We hadn't yet made it out of the tent as we speculated about the show we had just watched.

"Ah, my young ladies!" the master said. "And how did you enjoy the show, eh? She is most beautiful and graceful, no?" Tess and I agreed that it was really breathtaking. The master continued, "So, how do you like living in your Cobalt City? All of those heroes, quite a past indeed!"

"It does make for rather exciting news!" I said.

"And you, mademoiselles? Do you have special gifts and 'talents'?" He said with a wink and a playful smile

"Well, no, not really." Tess replied. "Though our parents are good friends with the Libertine. He's mysterious, and seems to have really strong mind-powers and can float through the air! Almost like the dancer!"

I thought that was bit too much information to give a stranger. I tried to subtly elbow Tess in the ribs.

"Indeed?" said Master Leschone, more serious now. "Has he shown up often in your life?"

"Actually, he—" Tess began, before I elbowed her again. Harder, this time.

"Not that often." I casually replied. But Master Leschone had a sharp look in his eye, like a hunting dog catching the scent. I knew Father was the Libertine, but Tess didn't. I knew that he would tell her when she was of a more mature age to know, as he had with me. Until then, I was one of a handful of people who knew Father's secret. "Anyway, we really ought to be going now." I had a tingling on the back of my neck, as I started to get a bad feeling about this man. Perhaps I had inherited some of my father's abilities to sense unnatural things.

"Of course, ladies. Perhaps, I will see you later," Master Leschone said as he watched us as we walked away.

"Hey, Natalie!" Tess whispered. "Let's go around back and meet that dancer. I want to get her autograph!"

"I don't know, Tess. I don't think everything is quite right here," I said slowly.

Tess grabbed my arm and kept insisting, arguing that it would only take a few minutes. She went inside the back of the tent, and having no choice, I followed.

Kamarina was brushing her hair in front of a tall oval mirror. She glanced over her shoulder at us, unsurprised to see us.

"Are you sisters?" she asked, eyeing us.

"Yes," I replied. "I'm Natalie, and this is Tess."

"How delightful," she said, putting down her brush. "What can I do for you?"

"We loved your performance!" Tess blurted out.

"Well, thank you. Please, won't you sit down?" She gestured to a couple of foldable camp chairs.

"Oh, no, no thank you," I replied. "We won't be staying long. It's just my sister wanted to-"

"Oooooh! Look at the beautiful costumes!" Tess squealed. "And these peacock feathers are luscious!" She ran her hands over the soft, lustrous feathers.

"There is a legend, you know," Kamarina said, "that peacock feathers, they are the eyes of the devil."

"Oh, that's silly," Tess said. "How could anything so lovely be so danger—*Ow!*"

I had a sharp sense of foreboding, like a trap had just snapped shut. "What is it, Tess?"

"Oh, nothing, I guess. There was something sharp here in the feathers, and it stuck my finger." She held out her hand, and sure enough, there was a small welling of blood on her fingertips.

Suddenly, Master Leschone swept into the tent. He, also, did not seem surprised to see us.

"Well done, Kamarina." He turned to her first. "You have upheld your end of the bargain."

"What exactly is going on here?" I demanded to know.

Kamarina turned to me. Her eyes were sad, and a little guilty, but her face was set. "I'm sorry, Natalie. I had no choice. You see, Leschone here, well, he has a hold on me, under a contract so to speak. I've been caught here for longer than I care to remember, and I want to leave. This dark carnival is…dangerous. Both for those of us caught in the web as performers, and the unwitting audiences. But the only way to leave is to find someone to take my place, or to die myself. I'm not ready to die, so, it had to be someone else. I want to go see the world and not from under the shadow of the carnival. It's a living death to do what I do."

"Tess? It had to be *Tess?*" I cried.

"Honestly," said Leschone, inspecting his fingernails. "I don't really care which of you it will be. But your sister has spilled her blood with the peacock feathers, and that commences a new, binding contract. However, since you share the same blood, I will let you two decide who will be Kamarina's replacement. If it makes a difference, your disabilities shall not present a problem. We have our ways of working around such things."

"This was all a trap, wasn't it?" I realized out loud. "Your performance caught my sister's mind and hooked us both! You— you do something while you're dancing, don't you?"

"Yes," Kamarina said simply. "I siphon off bits of their souls, without them even realizing it. Not enough to permanently damage them—but it weakens them, makes them more susceptible to the Dark Carnival. Master Leschone does something with this soul-energy, I don't know what or how exactly. But it comes down to souls, you see. Theirs, or mine. And now, yours or your sister's. I can't do it anymore. I just—I can't."

I looked over at Tess. She had gone pale, and was wringing her hands, smearing blood all around her knuckles. I loved my sister fiercely, but she was too high-strung to be able to handle a future serving in this demonic carnival. I took her by the shoulders, and looked straight into her eyes.

"Tess. Listen to me. I'm going to do this. No, don't argue, and don't cry, baby sister. You have a strong healthy body, and can live a full life. I don't have any future to lose. You need to go find Mother and Father, and tell them what's happened. Father will know what to do. Please."

Tess burst into tears, hugged me fiercely, one last time, and whispered "I'm so sorry, Nat!" She dashed out the door. I desperately hoped that our father, with his mental powers, would pick up on her distress and know where to come. I feared that Master Leschone's evil presence would jumble any distress call I could send out. Maybe over time I would find some way to work around that problem. And perhaps Father could still help…if he got here in time.

I brushed away my tears, settled my shoulders, and turned around. "What do I do now?"

It was the point of no return. Tess' blood had started the process, but my blood would finish it. I nicked my finger with a small ritual knife that Leschone handed me, and he sealed up the drops in a small vial, which he tucked into the inside pocket of his jacket. Kamarina directed me to the dressing area, where I was to change into my costume. The costume would give me the physical ability to perform. My first performance, sucking the souls from the audience, would put the final seal on my fate with the Carnaval Pomme D'or.

A very short time later, Kamarina was walking off alone into the sunset. My father had not arrived. Dressed and waiting in the wings, I prepared myself for my first act. Kamarina had assured me that I would be given the abilities I would need by Leschone to perform, as part of the deal. I got physical strength and grace, unending youth, all for the price of my captive soul and engaging with the audience to get their energy to supply the demonic forces that surrounded me.

And so I began my first performance with the Carnaval Pomme D'or. In the back of the audience, I saw my father dash into the tent. He had arrived too late.

Natalie looked up from her lap, where she had been staring at her hands. Her eyes were bright. "I found out much later, Tess was so hysterical it took our parents some time to get out of her what happened, and then for my father to get to the tent. Heroes back then were still developing their abilities. That first performance was the last time I saw my father. Years later, I heard that he had settled into a gradual retirement, and passed away quite some time ago. Master Leschone liked to torture me with this information—I don't know how he knew it, or whether any of it was even true. But he enjoyed the agony it brought me. Especially because of my legs, it keeps me trapped here. I have nowhere else to go, and no way to escape."

I reached over and took one of Natalie's hands. "Do you know, my grandmother's name was Tess?"

Natalie smiled sadly at me. "Then that means that I might be your great-aunt. It would be good to know that there are still people in my family continuing to help the people of Cobalt City."

"What can I do to help?" I asked.

"I'm not going to do what Kamarina did. I won't ask someone else to suffer this sort of half-life, being used by evil and sucking souls for a demon. There is only one other option."

I understood. "You need me to distract Leschone?"

She nodded. "Just long enough for me to do what I must. What I have in mind will be quick."

I gave her a quick, fierce hug, and stepped out of the tent. As the current Libertine of Cobalt City, and a reserve member of the Protectorate, I find myself involved in some of the city's spectacular supernatural events. Le Carnaval Pomme D'or would prove to be no exception. It would seem as though something that should be as innocuous as a carnival would hide no truly sinister intent—after all, they put their true freaks, fake magicians and unabashedly rigged games right out in the open. One would think the carnival had nothing to hide. But one would be wrong—after all, this *is* Cobalt City. And we do not attract anything tame.

I had thought to have a carefree and fun day at the fair with my friends. Instead I'd followed a mental pull of someone calling out specifically to me, and wondering if I was really following the right instinct. But now, having met Natalie and hearing her stories, validated those instincts, and gave me a certain amount of justification for taking on the mantle of the Libertine. It was in my blood.

I used my powers of illusion to change into the Libertine. With my mind, I settled the gold mask on my face, and attached the long cloak to hide my civilian clothes. I heard Master Leschone approaching and I could see him better now.

He wore what must have been the same outfit as when Natalie first saw him—a dark suit, tastefully accent with tiny mirrors on the jacket. Rather than looking tacky or gawdy, he carried them with panache. He also did not seem bothered by the evening heat, especially considering his dark suit.

I stepped out from the shadows of the tent. "Well met, Master Leschone."

I stepped into the shadowy interior of the Big Top, dressed in my costume.

He whirled around "Oh, a Cobalt City super-hero. How delightfully quaint. Run along now, child. You're out of your realm here." He dismissed me with a wave of his hand.

I smiled. "You have no idea of the definition of a super-hero, you demonic leech."

"You are wasting your time. There are no lives here to save."

"Who said a super-hero always saves the life?" I countered, as I began to circle him, trying to draw his attention away from the tents. "Sometimes there are things even more valuable to save."

I began to climb up the ropes of the trapeze, nearly to the ceiling.

Leschone sneered. "Please. You do-gooder types are all the same. Save the life of the victim, so on and so forth. Doesn't it get tiring?"

"One could make some sweeping generalizations about demonic lackeys too, Leschone." I said. "For example, I could presume that you of all people would know what I'm protecting right now."

"Oh? And what is that?" Leschone continued turning in place to face me as I circled him.

"A soul," I said.

"My soul," I thought, and let go.

Suddenly, the devil-in-disguise gasped and doubled over, looking pale and sick. "What—NO!" Leschone cried. He shot me a glare, then turned and looked at the large performance tent. Hobbling over, he clawed his way in through back entrance.

There, in the middle of the floor, lay Natalie's broken body, still highlighted by the spotlight from earlier and with dust motes swirling in the air from landing in the sawdust. She had climbed her way up the ropes of the trapeze, and then let herself go. It was quick and painless, it seemed, and she seemed to have a slight smile on her face. She was finally at peace and her soul was free.

"Thank you…" was my final thought, as I looked down on the scene below.

Leschone turned over his shoulder to hiss at me. "This isn't over, you know. One battle doesn't win a war, and the loss of one soul won't stop me forever. There are forces greater than I at work here, running this show. Even I don't know how deep the darkness goes. And Le Carnaval Pomme D'or will always be back again someday. It is inevitable."

He pushed past me and staggered into the night. He seemed to disappear, but perhaps that was just a trick of my eyes. The loss of Natalie and the power she brought with her performance had weakened him, but not forever. I knew he wasn't really gone—he would be back, the next time the carnival came to Cobalt City.

Ashley Bates was born in to a family that loves to read, and was infected with this incurable disease at a very young age by reading *Curious George & the Pizza*. The only known treatment to keep her happy is by constantly providing new and interesting books to read. There is no cure for the madness.

When not reading vociferously, Ashley enjoys romping with her Pomeranian, playing with fire in aesthetically pleasing ways, ruling her domicile as a domestic goddess and knitting with bamboo needles. And she really does want world peace!

Unexpected Sparx
Dawn Vogel

Kara Sparx groaned as she rolled out of bed. Sleeping on her guest bedroom mattress for a few days had made her realize just how horrible it was. With her sister and niece in town, Kara had decided the two of them should share the master suite, while she slept in the tiny downstairs bedroom ostensibly reserved for guests. Of course, Kara was the first person to sleep on the guest bed. Most of her old friends had a wide array of choices as to where they would stay when they visited Cobalt City. When family came, though, it only made sense to let them stay with her.

As Kara stretched and winced at the popping noises of her back, she noticed that the house seemed oddly quiet. She glanced at the clock and realized that she had slept nearly until noon. After waking up by eight the past two mornings, she guessed she needed the extra sleep. But she had been awoken on those mornings by her niece, Bridget. On the first morning, the seven-year-old girl had been digging through Kara's toolbox. The second morning, she had tried to hook up one of Kara's amplifiers. Bridget's mother, Denise, had managed to stop her daughter on both occasions, but the noise didn't let Kara sleep as late as she was accustomed to.

Kara reached for her cell phone and checked for messages. Finding none, she called Denise's cell phone, half listening to see if she could hear her sister's ridiculous pop song ringtone in the house.

"Hello?" Denise's voice was distorted by a heavy wind.

"Denise? Did you and Bridget go out?"

"Oh, yeah. We didn't want to wake you. Bridget kept seeing those carnival posters everywhere, and she promised to be extra quiet this morning if I took her."

Kara groaned inwardly. "Denise, I told you the carnival was a bad idea."

"I know, but you've seen how Bridget can get. I didn't want her to get into your stuff again. I figured we'd just get out of your hair and let you sleep late this morning. You've been a bit grumpy the last two mornings."

Kara bit the inside of her cheek to keep herself from responding too quickly. "Well thanks. I do appreciate the extra sleep. Tell you what, I'll meet you at the zoo in an hour?"

"Oh, that won't work. Bridget has her heart set on a puppet show at 1:30. Can you meet us here instead?"

Kara winced at the thought of a puppet show with more children like Bridget. "Yeah, I'll be there soon. Just need a shower and some coffee."

"Great, Kara! Bridget will be so glad you're going to join us. See you soon!"

Kara tossed her phone back onto her bedside table and rubbed her eyes. "Lumien?"

"Good morning, Kara." Her robot's voice came through an internal earpiece, as crisp as though he was standing in front of her.

"Denise took Bridget to the carnival. Do we have any new intel on it?"

"No reports have been filed at our clearance level—a situation which would be remedied if you became an active member of the Protectorate. However I have indications that several of the Protectorate have been running surveillance on the location for several days."

Kara toyed with the idea of calling a contact, but as she ran down the list of likely candidates, she decided that she wasn't quite ready to drag anyone else in yet. It was still hours until sunset, and the information she had gleaned about the last visit of the Le Carnaval Pomme D'or, mostly from the less-secure files of the Protectorate, suggested that the worst occurrences all took place after dark.

"Get my things together, Lumien. We're going to the carnival."

It took Kara a little longer than planned to get to the carnival. As she showered, she thought about how to explain to Denise and Bridget why they really shouldn't spend a lot of time at the carnival. She had already told Denise about the high rate of disappearances the last time the carnival came to Cobalt City. Denise, however, had chalked it up to lax parenting standards of the early 1980s. Kara bristled at the implication—she was still a few years shy of thirty, making her a child of the eighties. Denise was twelve years older than Kara, and the age difference was often apparent when they reminisced about their respective childhoods.

Kara and Lumien arrived at the carnival a little after one. Lumien had covered his brass exterior with a holographic projection of a broad-shouldered man with a toddler on each arm. Kara marveled sometimes at how good her robot was at blending in. Just as Kara was about to go over the game plan with Lumien, her cell phone rang. "Hi, Denise. Just got here."

"Oh, good! I don't know how much longer we can save you a seat at the puppet show."

"Right, puppet show." Kara scanned the map of the carnival grounds. Lumien pointed to the location on the map before she could spot it on her own. "Thanks, Lu…" Realizing she was still connected to Denise, she cut herself off. "I'll be right there."

She hung up the phone and looked imploringly at Lumien. "Sometimes I wish that you were able to get sick. Then I'd have an excuse to get out of family visits."

Lumien looked at Kara quizzically. "Should I feign illness?"

"No, no. Just take a walk around. Try to find any hidden exits, in case we need to get out of here quickly. I'm not fond of the thought that there's only one way in or out."

"Of course, Kara."

Kara turned and headed in the direction of the puppet show. At every turn, she ignored the carnival barkers trying to lure unsuspecting patrons into their tents. Kara possessed no special way of sensing danger, but she knew that this place was giving her the creeps. In the daylight, it was the most polished carnival she had ever been to. The tents were bright and colorful, showing no signs of fading or patching. The air was heavy with scents of kettle corn and cotton candy, but without the underlying smell of vomit that usually accompanied carnival rides. By all outward appearances, this could have been one of the happiest places on earth. And that made Kara even more wary.

The only sound that caused her any alarm was the creaking of the Ferris wheel as it slowly rotated. A screech like two pieces of metal rubbing against one another pierced Kara's ears. She looked over toward the Ferris wheel and watched the ride operator, a hunchbacked elderly man, bang on the support beam that stabilized the ride. The screeching noise subsided as quickly as it had begun.

Reaching the puppet show, Kara bought her ticket and pushed past the heavy canvas flap of the tent. Out of the corner of her eye, she thought she saw a Chihuahua-sized creature scurry away. The dim lighting of the tent prevented her from seeing details more clearly, but she noticed a handful of soccer moms with purse dogs in the audience.

Before Kara could investigate further, Denise waved to her. Kara made her way down, moving carefully so as not to jostle any of the other patrons. She wore her leather jacket a little larger than necessary to conceal the rocket pack strapped to her back. Bumping into anyone would draw attention to the sizeable metallic mass.

"Hi, Auntie Kara," Bridget exclaimed as Kara sat down. "Aren't you excited to see the puppets?"

Kara glanced at the small puppet stage at one end of the tent. "Yeah, I'm sure it'll be really great, Bridget."

Bridget turned around and settled into her seat. Denise leaned closer to Kara. "Who's Lou?"

Kara arched one eyebrow, preparing to respond, when the audience erupted into applause. The lights in the tent dimmed, and a pair of puppets appeared on the stage, lit by the harsh white light of a single spotlight. "Saved by the puppets," she muttered.

"Oh no, you're not," Denise whispered with a sly smile.

Kara grimaced, partially at her sister and partially at the poorly piped-in music that accompanied the puppet show. The speakers distorted the sound nearly beyond recognition, but it sounded like a warped version of "Pop Goes the Weasel." Somehow, all of the children in the audience were entranced, while most of the adults in the audience were glued to their smartphones. Denise, however, focused her attention on Kara.

"What? Aren't you going to watch the puppets?" Kara asked.

"No, I want to hear about your friend, Lou."

"Lou?"

"When we were on the phone, you said 'Thanks, Lou.' So who is he? Or is it a she? Boyfriend? Girlfriend?"

Kara laughed, a far harsher sound than she had anticipated. "God, no, Denise." Then she paused, trying to figure out how to explain her robot to her sister. Lumien hadn't been out of the lab since Denise and Bridget had arrived, and Kara had simply waved past the door when she gave them the tour of her house, muttering something about the basement being a mess. "Look, can we talk about this later?"

"We're here now," Denise replied.

Kara sighed. The repetitive music was getting on her nerves, but she saw no easy escape. "Fine. Lou is short for, umm, Lucien. He's just a friend."

Denise smiled knowingly. "You say that now, but just you wait."

"You're like those people who talk in the theater, sis. Special hell. Shut up and watch the puppets."

Kara stood outside the puppet show tent with Denise and Bridget after the show. "So, ready for the zoo?"

"No way," Bridget said with a stomp of her foot. "Mom bought me a bunch of ride tickets. Mom, can I hold them?"

Denise dug through her purse and handed her daughter a wad of red tickets. "Put them in your pocket, honey." Bridget instead began to count the tickets, and Denise turned her attention back to Kara. "So, Lucien…"

"Mo-oomm," Bridget interrupted. "I have fifteen ride tickets."

"Not now, honey. Auntie Kara and I are having grown-up time."

Bridget rolled her eyes, looking every bit like her mother's daughter. Kara had only been a toddler when Denise was a teenager, but she remembered her sister's attitude. She wasn't surprised that Bridget had picked it up.

"So, is he European?"

Kara laughed. "No, not exactly. Maybe a little bit Swiss, but he's not really from there."

"Swiss, huh? That sounds exotic."

"What would it take for me to convince you that Lucien and I are only friends? There's nothing there."

"Mom, I'm bored. Can I go ride the rides now?" Bridget peered up at her mother hopefully.

Denise sighed, ignoring her daughter. "Okay. But Kara, sweetie, I just think it's time for you to settle down with a nice guy. Or girl, whichever."

"Really? If I remember right, sis, that didn't work out so well for you." Kara wished she had bitten her tongue as soon as the words were out of her mouth.

Denise looked crestfallen. "You know, do as I say, not as I do. I just want you to be happy."

"I think I'm happier on my own, sis."

"I guess. But you know it would make Mom and Dad happy too. They're not as young as they once were. Mom's been talking about wanting a big Christmas again. Lots of cousins and kids running around, like it was when you were little."

Kara tried not to roll her eyes, but her arms crossed almost involuntarily as she tried to end the discussion. She turned her head away from Denise and noticed that Bridget was no longer standing near them. "Where's Bridget?"

Denise spun around, frantically looking for her daughter. Kara scanned the area more slowly, but the crowds were thick around them. Soundlessly, she channeled her thoughts into the communication system between herself and Lumien. "Lumien, Bridget has disappeared. Tell me you got that tracker implanted in her sneaker before she left?"

"Yes, it is installed and functional. Bridget appears to be approximately 20 feet above the surface of the Earth at present."

Kara shifted her gaze upwards and spotted the Ferris wheel. She grabbed Denise by the arm and pointed. "She's up there."

"Bridget!" Denise exclaimed. "Why on earth would the ride operator let a seven year old on the Ferris wheel by herself?"

Kara shrugged, but Denise stalked off toward the ride, ready to give the elderly carnie a piece of her mind. Kara hung back and watched the giant wheel spin. For as new as the ride looked, the motion was not nearly as smooth as she would have expected. Brow furrowing, she pulled her goggles from an interior pocket and put them on. "Lumien, I'm sending you a feed from the Ferris wheel. Can you run it through the optics?"

"Of course, Kara." A moment passed before he spoke again. "Kara, there seems to be a growing level of energy at the center of the mechanism."

As Lumien spoke, Kara watched the wheel stop moving and shift downward. Without warning, one of the legs on either side of the Ferris wheel pulled free of the ground and began writhing, snakelike.

"The energy appears to have peaked," Lumien reported.

"I'll say. We've got trouble. I'm going to need some crowd control." Kara shrugged out of her jacket and tossed it at a nearby onlooker. "Hang on to that for me, will you?" The young man was staring at the Ferris wheel, a look of horror on his face.

Kara shook her head and flipped the thrusters on her rocket pack into action.

Kara flew upwards, keeping her distance from the flailing legs of the Ferris wheel. Each broad sweep of the appendages cleared a slightly broader space, as the assembled crowds tried to run. From the air, Kara could see the likely source of the energy that had animated the Ferris wheel—the top of the axle was crackling with sickly green energy.

The caged car holding Bridget and a few other children was near the top of the Ferris wheel. Kara flew a little closer so that she could get a good look at the mechanism that held the door closed. The entire Ferris wheel shook as the free legs tugged at the two legs that were still stationary. It looked like it was trying to free itself from quicksand.

Adjusting the focus on her goggles, Kara used the zoom lens to provide a clearer view of the lock. "Lumien, I'm sending you a picture of the locking mechanism. I need to know the fastest way to get it open."

Lumien responded almost immediately. "It is an electronic bolting mechanism. A brief burst from your zap gun should disengage the lock."

Kara swooped down towards the cars that were only a few feet off the ground. "Stand clear of the door," she announced to the passengers, leveling one of her zap guns at the lock. The passengers crowded to the opposite side, and she unleashed a quick blast. The mechanism hummed, followed by a click. "Go. Get out of there and move away from the Ferris wheel." A middle-aged woman took the children by the hand and hurried out the open door.

Kara moved toward the next car, but found her way impeded by a flailing Ferris wheel leg. She rocketed upwards, passing the car that Bridget was trapped in. "Aunt Kara!" The girl called out.

Kara waved at her niece dismissively. "Not now. I'm a little busy." She looked at Bridget, trying to muster up a smile. "I'll get you out of there. Promise."

As she turned her attention back to the animated ride, she spotted one of the legs flying directly towards her. She dodged to her left, her right shoulder clipping the frame of the caged car that Bridget was in. She released hold on the zap gun in that hand, and heard it clatter off of the bars of the cage.

Before she could locate where it had fallen, the other leg swung at her, coming perilously close to the cage. "Lumien? I need help. Can you keep one of the legs occupied? I need this thing to stop swinging at me so I can get the passengers out."

"Affirmative," Lumien chirped. Kara couldn't see what her robot was up to, but one of the legs was no longer anywhere near the cages. She took off in the other direction, flying in the sorts of loops and spirals that she normally saved for paying customers who had hired her to put on an aerial show.

In the distance, Kara heard a pulse fired from her missing zap gun. She scanned the ground, trying to find it. She noticed a few small dark spots on the ground, which seemed to be heading in Lumien's direction. Before she could warn him, she saw that the door to Bridget's cage was hanging open. The girl was shimmying down one of the spokes toward the center of the Ferris wheel.

Kara cursed under her breath and started toward the thin spoke. The Ferris wheel swung at her, blocking her movement towards her niece. "Oh, now you're just making me mad." She fired off an ineffectual blast from her remaining zap gun, watching as the electricity skittered across the surface of the leg. A small shriek from Bridget was just loud enough to draw Kara's attention. The girl was still crawling down the spoke, but she waved one of her hands back and forth. Kara could just make out a scorch mark across her palm.

"Lumien, don't hit it with anything electrical. It conducts."

"Indeed," Lumien said, sounding slightly rattled. "I just received a bit of a shock myself."

"Alright, get ready. I need you to run through the center when I fly through to get Bridget. And 5, 4, 3…"

Before Kara could finish her countdown, she heard the swirling calliope of carnival music. She paused, watching as the wheel began to turn slowly. Bridget had reached the axle and had perched on the end of it. She fired a beam of electricity downward, aiming for a gap in the loading platform. Two of the cages moved onto the loading platform, and Bridget stopped.

Kara grinned from ear to ear, and fired off two quick shots to unlock the doors of the cars. Bridget turned her head slightly, and Kara could see that the girl's facial expression matched hers.

"Scratch that, Lumien. Just keep the thing distracted while we get the passengers out."

Bridget continued to rotate the Ferris wheel to move more occupied cars into the unloading position. Kara began flying long, lazy ellipsoid shapes to keep the animated Ferris wheel occupied and get herself into the right position to unlock the doors as soon as Bridget had cars in position. The two of them made quick work of the job, and Kara flew up towards her niece.

"Not bad, kiddo. Now let's get you out of here." She stretched out her arms to the girl.

"Aunt Kara, watch out!" Bridget exclaimed. Too late, Kara turned to see one of the legs plow into her midsection. As the air escaped her lungs, the rocket pack sputtered, threatening to stall. She regained enough of her senses to steer herself towards a nearby tent, but the impact was nearly as bad as it would have been had she hit the ground.

"Lumien?" she croaked.

"I am having a bit of unanticipated difficulty at the moment, Kara. I will get to you as soon as I can."

"Unanticipated difficulty?"

"Yes, Kara. At the moment, there are puppets attached to all of my appendages. They have drained my power capacity to less than 40 percent."

"I guess jolting them isn't an option then." She thought for a moment, lifting herself up on her elbows to survey the scene. Bridget clutched the axle as tightly as she could while staying away from the strange energy there. Lumien was, as he said, covered in small dark shapes that looked a lot like the thing Kara had spotted earlier at the puppet show. "Wait. Get as close to the Ferris wheel as you can. It's got way more power than you do. Get the puppets to attack it!"

Lumien's voice sounded tired, like a record played too slowly. "Yes, Kara."

Kara braced herself and rose to her knees. Every inch of her body hurt, but she had enough self-control to pilot the rocket pack. She hoped she would have enough strength to safely transport her niece to the ground. Falling would not be an option with a seven year old girl clinging to her.

She watched as Lumien wrapped his arms around the remaining leg on his side of the Ferris wheel. Instantly, the puppets released their hold on him and began scurrying up towards the axle. Kara activated her rocket pack and flew towards Bridget.

"Bridget, you crawled down that spoke and didn't fall. I need you to hold on to me just as tight."

Bridget nodded solemnly, tucking the zap gun back into the holster on Kara's chest. She slung her arms around Kara's neck and squeezed her knees around Kara's hips. One of the Ferris wheel's legs flailed in their direction, but fell short. Kara still didn't want to take any chances. She flew away from the Ferris wheel twice as far as the legs could reach and landed, carefully lowering Bridget to the ground.

"Is your robot going to be okay?" Bridget asked.

"How did you…oh, I guess he can't hide himself right now. He'll be fine." Kara glanced up and noticed Denise rushing in their direction. "Here comes your mom."

"Bridget! Kara!" Denise exclaimed. "Are you alright?"

"We're fine, Mom," Bridget replied. "Aren't we, Aunt Kara?"

"Thanks to you," Kara admitted. She looked at Denise. "You've got yourself a little Sparx, that's for sure."

Dawn Vogel has been published as a non-fiction editor and as a short fiction writer. Her academic background is in history, so it's not surprising that most of her fiction is set in earlier times. She works as a historical researcher, traveling and seeing the sights all over the country with her nose buried in dusty old records. In her alleged spare time, she runs a craft business, helps officiate roller derby (on and off skates), and tries to find time for writing. She lives in Seattle with her awesome husband and fellow author Jeremy and their herd of cats.

Now You See Me, Now You Don't
Amber Keller

Mister Grey loved the night. Subtle overhead lamps lit the streets, shadows moved alone in the darkest corners, and the moon was high overhead, shining brightly in its fullness. Apart from an occasional straggler, there usually wasn't anyone else on his walk back home after leaving a gig this late, and that was the way he liked it. He had no body in the traditional sense, only this conglomerate of ash given form by dark magic and force of will alone. He felt a freedom and comfort with the nighttime.

As he walked down the darkened alley, a huge, bald man crossed where it intersected the main road. The man held a roll of papers in his hand and did not look down the alley. Mister Grey stopped, curious. After he was out of sight, Mister Grey quietly ran up the side of the alley, in the shadows, and peered around the corner. The man put up a poster on the closest light pole, and moved on to the next. Grey looked back and saw them plastered on walls, windows, and poles, flapping in a light breeze. They all carried the same message—Le Carnaval Pomme D'or was coming to town.

Time to visit Wild Kat.

The Marco Polo was always a bittersweet reminder of his grim past, but tonight there was too much on his mind to let emotions creep in.

"Kat," Grey said. She turned at the sound of his voice.

"Simon, it's so nice to see you," she said as she reached out to briefly touch his gloved hand. Her voice purred his name.

"My pleasure, as always." His low voice spoke softly. "I have come to speak to you about the imminent arrival of the carnival."

"I was just speaking to some of the others. This is a dangerous situation. Our protector services will be needed."

Wild Kat paced as she spoke, her black leather pants shining in the moonlight.

"I will be paying a visit to see what I can uncover about their intentions," Grey said.

"You will rely on us for help, if it's needed, won't you?" Concern flashed quickly through her eyes. "What I mean is stay safe, friend. Cobalt City lost some good people the last time, and I do not want to see it happen on my watch."

Her phone rang, prompting her to answer.

Grey nodded and left. He could hear her voice as he descended the stairs. The situation was unnerving.

He watched for them to arrive. On the second night, his waiting paid off. A caravan of trucks pulled into a lot on the outskirts of Cobalt City. Within moments people piled out of the vehicles, unpacking equipment and setting up. Grey dissolved his human form, turned to a cloud of ash to move in for a closer view.

People of all sizes moved about with practiced precision to assemble the great structures, while beyond his field of vision the Ferris wheel had already started going up as if by magic. Grey moved fluidly in between the trucks and tents, dispersing his ash so that no one would notice him. He listened for any talk of the malevolent reason behind their visit, but gleaned no information.

The acts were similar to previous recorded visits, though the names had changed. He saw a woman whose face appeared to be covered with fur. Her nose was prominent and pointy. A man with scaly skin sat in a large tub of water with his legs fused together to form a rudimentary tail. The truck next to him sported a painted side boasting 'Icthus the Fish-man'.

The sideshow acts, or the freaks, were always an integral part of the show. With his unique circumstances, Grey thought, it wasn't so hard to imagine himself being put on display. The ash particles shuddered in a wave briefly as this went through his thoughts. Suddenly a voice came from behind him.

"You. I know you're there." A man, remarkably plain at first glance pointed right at Mister Grey. It was when the second voice sounded, croaked from a malformed mouth on the back of this man's head that Mister Grey recognized the speaker: Unfortunate John the Two-faced Oracle. "I've a message for you."

As the second, foul lips spoke, his primary mouth hung slack and mute. His face twitched, and his eyes blinked. His face carried a tortured quality. Grey stayed silent.

"The oracle speaks of darkness to come, days of violence and despair. On Cobalt City the sun will shine no more."

Grey wasn't one to listen to prophecies; however, an undefined power emanating from the soothsayer began to dominate his logical thinking. Images flashed across his mind of destruction. He saw the citizens of Cobalt City, but they were different, somehow changed.

The primary face seemed to gain control. The eyes were possessed by sad certainty. "Your days are numbered, strange one." His voice had grown shrill and loud.

Another man wearing a red turban and cloak appeared beside the soothsayer. Mister Grey realized he needed to get out of there before more people discovered him.

Willing all of his ash to dissipate and reappear outside of the carnival grounds, he left. As he moved he saw the soothsayer's primary face speaking in tongues and the man beside him crossed his arms and gave rise to a long, low, sinister laugh.

When Mister Grey reached the city, the laugh was still echoing through his head.

The next night, as Mister Grey left the lost subway station he called home, one of his informants approached him.

"Mister Grey, there's something you oughta know about." The man had a gravelly voice, and his clothes smelled from the stench of filth. A blackened baseball hat was pulled down toward his eyes, one of which was offset and wandered to the side, and his cheeks were smeared with dirt. He kept his hands in his pockets and walked quickly. He was one of the Perdido Street Irregulars.

They ducked into the nearest alleyway and stood near a dumpster.

"What have you got?" asked Grey.

"Well, you see, Harold told me late last night that some strange folk had been scouring the streets for drak, that new drug that hit Cobalt City last month. They seem to want as much as they can get their hands on. They came up to him and it scared him a bit, you see, their looks." He looked over his shoulder from time to time as he spoke, nervously watching the quiet streets.

"Did you see any of them?"

"I did. Just two. One was real short, came up a little over my knee." He put his hand on his leg to show how tall he meant. "They were both dressed in strange clothes."

Mister Grey thought a minute. They could be carnies, and the fact that they were looking for drugs in such quantity couldn't be good news.

"Were they able to find any drak?" asked Grey.

"Yeah, I heard they did score quite a bit. You're always so determined to get drugs off the street. This sounded like something you might want to know about."

"You did the right thing. Thank you for coming to find me." Grey reached into his pocket and gave the man some money. "You look hungry, my friend. Go eat."

The man took the money and shoved it into his pocket. Times were hard, and a good meal was hard to come by for some.

"Thank you, Mister Grey. Thank you." He moved as if to give Grey a hug then considered his patron's insubstantial form.

Mister Grey clapped him softly on the shoulder and nodded for him to go.

Now he needed to get to the bottom of this. The carnival folk looking for large amounts of drak was concerning. Drak was one of the newest drugs to hit the street. It was powerful and not one to be played with. The effects of drak were mind numbing and would give the user a feeling of invincibility. People on it had been known to cause lethal injuries to others, for their strength was temporarily heightened. If the carnies were users, that was one thing, but looking to buy all of it didn't add up.

He had seen the damage drugs caused firsthand. The love of his life had been a heroin junkie and her addiction had played a central role in turning him into the ashen form he had been trapped in following his brutal death. In his supernaturally extended afterlife, Mister Grey made it his personal crusade to try and eliminate drugs from Cobalt City, and now it seemed that the carnival was scouring the streets for drak. He would have to find out for sure.

There would be another trip to the carnival tonight.

Walking through the parked cars, Grey joined the crowds of Cobalt City citizens to enter the carnival. The grass was trampled down, the last rays of sun had set only moments before, and the stars were blinking into view. People formed a line to pay the ticket master. Multi-colored lights dotted the landscape, and the rides moved with no one on them. The great Ferris wheel loomed in the near distance, watching over them all. The smell of cotton candy and popcorn wafted through the air. Along with the traditional sights, there was a pull, an undercurrent that gave off an electrical feel. There was so much more than just a carnival happening here.

As Grey scanned over the crowd, he noticed that the people had glazed eyes, and flowed in unison toward the entrance. Magic was most certainly being used, and he was immune to its effects.

Breaking away from the crowd, he slid through a curtain. Once inside, he began following some workers who were talking about going to see the ringmaster. Someone in charge could be just who he was looking for. He followed behind them in the shadows. They approached a large tent and lifted a flap to duck in. He followed after them into the darkness of the tent.

There were stacks of crates and boxes to one side, perfect for hiding behind. Beyond the crates was a large open space. The room had a soft glow from the few temporary lights that were set up. It was warm and humid beneath the canvas. In the corner of the room, the ringmaster stood stirring a giant pot. It was the same ringmaster from their last visit, with the black suit and red turban. Mister Grey would not forget that man.

Looking up from his work, the ringmaster stepped away when he saw the workers. They grabbed long sticks leaning against the tent wall and dipped them into the pot to begin stirring.   The sound of liquid sloshing brought the attention of the ringmaster.

"Careful, you fools, we don't want to lose any," said the ringmaster.

The men looked down and concealed angry faces.

A dwarf entered the tent. Hobbling over to the ringmaster, he held out his hand, which contained a clear glass bottle with a cork in the top.

"I have it, sir," said the dwarf.

"This is all you could find?" The ringmaster held up the bottle.

"Yes, sir, that was everything the city had." He looked at his feet as he said this.

"It should be enough. All we have to do now is add this to the mixture and distribute it into the drinks, the cotton candy, and snow cones. Our magic will make them irresistible. The citizens will be scrambling to acquire the treats. It's the perfect plan!"

"Yes, sir, of course, sir"

The ringmaster walked to a small table and set the bottle down. Turning, he stepped back to Sam.

"Remember, when they ingest it, we will have to work quickly to set our intentions. With their minds weak, we will insert the suggestion to kill each other. Next, we let them loose in the city, and Cobalt City will never be the same. By the time they can get it under control, the drug will be wearing off. The chaos and death that follow will never be forgotten, carrying our name to new heights of power and fear."

Mister Grey had to stop this and there was no time to call for help. The mixture could not make it into the mouths of the citizens. He was a protector, and as such it was his job to make sure this did not happen.

Acting quickly, Mister Grey disappeared only to reappear between the two workers. Stunned, they yelled and jumped back for a moment. Pushing with all of his strength, he began to tip the pot over.

"What the devil?" cried the ringmaster.

The men scrambled to right the pot, but it was too late. Mister Grey gave it one last kick and the pot fell over, the contents spilling out all over the floor.

"Grab it! Scoop it up!" The ringmaster advanced, snatching one worker by the neck of his shirt. As they fought to retrieve the drink, Grey dispersed and reappeared by the small table. Grabbing the bottle, he heard his name.

"Grey! You thief! I will kill you with my bare hands!" The ringmaster shouted and kicked the men as he scrambled to get to Mister Grey.

"You'll have to catch me first," said Grey.

He lunged towards Mister Grey, grabbing with his desperate hands. Grey scattered himself to the wind, carrying the bottle toward the exit. The ringmaster fell face down on the floor.

"I will destroy you. Mark my words. I will end you!" yelled the ringmaster.

Ash burst outward as he disappeared. The bottle was carried away on a cloud of semi-coherent ash, floating between the legs of the patrons, unseen. He moved quickly, fluidly, until he was far enough away to guarantee his escape.

Later that night, in the backstreets of Cobalt City, Mister Grey stood alone at a metal trashcan filled with flames. He uncorked the bottle and poured it into the fire.

Black smoke poured forth momentarily along with a sizzle and pop, then it was gone.

He looked into the fire. It had been fire that had turned him to ash so many years ago. He had been told his days were numbered, and the ringmaster vowed to kill him. These threats didn't scare him. He was already dead, after all. But the threats did serve to make him think. Being the only one of his kind brought with it the uncertainty of his future.

Mister Grey stayed there watching the fire for a long time that night. The flames licked up, the smoke floated away on the breeze. He had saved the citizens and a large quantity of a dangerous drug had been taken off the streets. A smile crept over his face. Tonight, Cobalt City would be a safer place.

Amber Keller is a writer from Tennessee who delves into such genres as horror, thriller, and fantasy. She has her poetry published, along with one book under a pen name, as well as several short stories that are out for submissions. Currently she has finished a horror novel, and is working on another. She is a member of the Horror Writers Association and Savvy Authors, and watches horror and science fiction movies to review for http://www.thegaspfactor.com. Her love of horror and things that go bump in the night began as a child. When not writing, she can be found participating in paranormal investigations and scouting out creepy locations for inspiration. Many of her short stories can be found on her blog, http://www.adiaryofawriter.blogspot.com.

Fortunes for the Brave Heart
Rosemary Jones

The air filled with the spicy scent of sizzling hot dogs, the delicious whiff of frying doughnuts, and the buttery burnt smoke of fresh popcorn, all underlaid with the subtle sweetness of sticky children clutching caramel apples or cotton candy.

Excited couples on dates swung by, arguing whether they should try the sideshow tents first or seek passage on the boats swinging through The Haunted Tunnel of Love. A red-haired woman laughed up at her stocky date as he draped a lazy arm across her shoulders and teased her with a sugary doughnut plucked from a white paper bag.

Teenagers pushed and shoved in their own group mating dance. At the other end of the spectrum, an elderly pair fell into amiable wrangling over who was the best shot at the rifle booth and who always won the most prizes.

Katherine Wilde felt her inner feline sit up and sniff hungrily at the tasty toddlers being pushed or pulled by frazzled parents searching out the sparkly rides at the Golden Apple Carnival. "Down, kitty," she muttered. Now was not the time for a snack—nor were fat babies ever appropriate food for her inner tiger.

She hated carnivals. Even with all her feline senses stuffed under her seemingly normal human exterior, the noise, the smells, the flashing lights, it all made her twitchy. If she had had a tail, it would be lashing from side to side. As it was, she struggled to keep her canines from descending into sharp points and curled her fingers into her palms to prevent instinctively swiping with razor-sharp claws at the next person who jostled her.

She wished she hadn't come, but she'd heard stories all week about strange happenings at the Golden Apple Carnival. Trouble had come to Cobalt City, disguised as a fun fair, and she needed to keep her wits and not be distracted by the memories dredged up by the smells and sounds of this carnival.

A dreadful night in Switzerland…a girl running down a dark mountain road to the brilliant lights and calliope music…

A dare sent young Katherine to the carnival. The expensive Swiss finishing school that her parents decreed necessary after the hat incident at Ascot had a nighttime curfew, of course. But even then, she'd been a bit of daredevil, a bit of an acrobat. She hadn't needed enhanced feline powers to unlatch an upper storey window and climb down a drainpipe.

It began as a bet with her roommate Claudine, that she could get out and visit Le Carnaval Pomme D'or and see all the wonders promised on the posters plastered throughout the village. The most intriguing one showed a two-faced man with slips of paper spilling from his fingers. Across the bottom was written: "*audentes fortuna iuvat.*" Being overly educated young ladies, she and her classmates were certain that they were the brave, the audacious, that fortune would favor. As the daughters of aristocrats, the wealthy, and the famous, they had every right to expect the world's riches to fall into their eagerly outstretched and perfectly manicured hands.

The beautiful Claudine, the daughter of an equally beautiful and chic former model, spent her nights whispering about the fortuneteller. "I want to know how wonderful my life will be," she told Katherine once.

"What will you do if you don't like your fortune?" Kat could never resist teasing Claudine, trying to ruffle the other girl's self-possession.

But the swift reaction startled her.

"Oh, if I was not going to be famous, I would die!" Claudine said.

104

The school wasn't a prison—they regularly took trips to theaters, museums, and other amusements. But Katherine still remembered the ripple of shock that ran through the assembly when, just hours before the carnival was to open, the headmistress flatly announced that no girl in her care was to visit it, that even attempting to see it would be grounds for expulsion.

And, of course, Katherine ranted about this ridiculous curtailment of their freedom to Claudine. She never meekly accepted the dictates of others—that quirk of her personality led to the disaster with the Queen Mother's hat, among other things.

"If you are so bold," Claudine said finally, "why don't you go?"

"I'll go, and I'll ride every ride," Katherine recklessly promised. "And I'll bring you back a prize from one of the booths."

"Bring me back my fortune," Claudine insisted. "One of those slips of paper."

"I will." Katherine never stopped to consider that she was taking all risks. If caught, she, and not Claudine, would be expelled.

So, later that night, she slipped between the black curtains of the fortuneteller's tent and met a small, remarkably plain little man, seated on a folding stool behind a simple wooden table. On the table—and this memory burned strangely clear in her mind— was a clay bowl filled to the brim with slips of folded paper.

"Take one," said the man and she'd been startled that he spoke English to her, not the more common French or German. "Take it and give it to me."

She'd plucked a strip of paper from the bowl and handed it across the table.

He had unfolded it and spent a long time staring, until she began to squirm under the pressing weight of his silence.

"*Cave felem.*" His face was blank and the sound came from everywhere and nowhere. For a moment, she was scared but then she told herself that it was only a ventriloquist's trick.

"Beware the cat?" Katherine translated from the Latin, showing off her expensive education.

He nodded. "If you do not take control of it, it will devour all. Even you."

"What nonsense!" she retorted. "I thought you told fortunes, predicted the future."

"I have," he answered. "Next time I can only tell you your past."

"That's foolish," the seventeen-year-old Katherine retorted. "Completely bonkers. Who wants to know their past?"

"You will. Some day. But now you must leave."

He stood up then and crossed the tent to hold the curtain open for her. The glare of the midway lights outside created a crooked shadow man against the far wall of the tent. The shadow had two faces: one looking forward and one looking back.

Katherine pretended to fumble with her purse, dropping an extra 50-franc note to upon the table and, at the same time, filching one of the paper fortunes from the bowl for Claudine.

"You needn't steal one," said the little man.

Startled, she swung to face him.

"Tell Claudine to heed her fortune if she wants to keep her future," he said.

Outside, the music blared through loudspeakers strung up in the trees and atop tent poles. The crowd shrieked in a babble of languages that made her want to clap her hands to her ears. Strangers swirled around her, shouting and pointing at the garish entertainments, and suddenly she wanted to leave. The carnival wasn't fun at all—it was hectic, and bewildering, and everyone seemed desperately hungry for something that they could never have.

For the first time in her life, and for the last, Katherine fled before her vague fears. She ran up the dark mountain road, escaping the maniacal confusion. She clawed her way up the drainpipe and fell, panting, into the moonlit bedroom.

"What took you so long?" asked Claudine from her bed, switching on a small bedside lamp and sitting up. "Did you get it? Did you?"

"Here," said Katherine, dropping the paper fortune on her lap. "I stole this for you." She didn't quite dare to admit that the strange fortuneteller had caught her in the act or tell Claudine his words of warning.

The French girl reached out her hands and unfolded the paper. "*Fortuna vitrea est; tum cum splendet, frangitur,*" she read. Her face was puzzled. Latin had never been Claudine's favorite subject.

But Katherine recognized the motto. They had spent a long and weary hour dissecting it in class. "Fortune is like glass, when it glitters, it breaks."

Claudine stared at her blankly when she translated it, and then, with a cry, crumpled the paper and tossed it away .

"That's horrid," she said.

"Well, it's your future," said Katherine, dropping exhausted onto her own bed.

"I don't want it," wept Claudine, her sudden sobs shaking her slim body. Footsteps pounded down the hallway, attracted by the girl's mounting hysteria.

The bedroom door was thrust open, followed shouts, alarms, and accusations of rules broken and curfews confounded. In the end, Katherine returned to England in disgrace. Claudine left the school a few months later.

A year after gracing the cover of the French *Vogue*, Claudine was found dead in her Paris apartment, the victim of an overdose. Recently embarked on the genetic modifications that would turn her into Wild Kat, Katherine only learned of Claudine's death while reading an ancient gossip magazine one night to distract herself from the pain and insomnia created by the beginning transformation of her body. In the obituary, some young writer decided to get fancy and quote an obscure Latin phrase, talking about a glittering career shattered by the emotional fragility of the unfortunate Claudine.

In the darkened waiting room, Katherine could not suppress a shudder. Was the paper slip that she gave Claudine merely a chance prediction or had it been a curse that set the girl's feet on the path to ruin?

Unlike Claudine, Kat mastered the fate thrust upon her by the fortuneteller. The cat did not consume her. But, sometimes, she dreamed she heard a calliope whistle and a strange voice whisper, "You still have a fortune waiting. Do you dare to hear it?"

Years later, the Cobalt City carnival shattered the night with its noise. In the middle of it, Katherine stood frozen, staring at a poster advertising Unfortunate John the Two-faced Oracle, a small man with slips of paper dropping like petals from his outstretched fingertips. A feline snarl escaped Katherine's curled lips. It couldn't be true. Yet it looked like the same man who ruined poor Claudine with his paper slip of a curse.

Intent on finding the fortuneteller, Katherine stalked down the narrow alley of the carnival's sideshows, searching past Questo the Mentalist, Ice Hair Tom, The China Doll Family, and Sateen the Razor Dancer for the fortuneteller's tent. Pushing past her, several couples headed for the Haunted Tunnel of Love, where they were promised the ride of a lifetime.

"Excuse me," a red-haired young woman clutched at Katherine's arm. "But can you help me?"

"I'm sorry. Do I know you?" To her own ears, her clipped vowels sounded terribly unfriendly. Kat softened her words with a quick and slightly apologetic smile.

"No, no, it's just…" The redhead swayed where she stood, her pale complexion turning almost ghostly under the garish neon of the carnival lights. Katherine glanced around and spotted a bench near Questo's tent. She guided the woman over and sat down beside her.

"Are you ill? Should I call someone?"

"No, I'm OK, at least, I think I am," her companion said. "It's just…well…this is going to sound so weird…but I think I lost someone. I think I lost someone important." Tears started to well in her large green eyes.

Katherine dug into the pocket of her leather jacket and pulled out a large, clean handkerchief, one of the most important tools that any super-hero (or heroine) could carry. She thrust it into the hands of the redhead and said, "Tell me what is wrong. But, first, blow."

With a hiccup, the young woman blew her nose and mopped her eyes.

"You're so nice, and I'm sorry, I never meant to stop you. You must think I'm crazy." She straightened up a little and thrust out her hand to Katherine. "I'm Berry, Berry Fields…it's Strawberry, really, my Mom was a bit of a Beatles freak…but everyone calls me Berry…even…." She trailed off and sat staring at Katherine. The tears continued to pour unheeded down her face.

"Even who?" prompted Katherine.

"That's it," said Berry, "I don't know. Except I do know. I know it is somebody important. Somebody who calls me Berry and buys doughnuts." She reached into the large satchel purse slung at her side and pulled out a crumpled bag of carnival doughnuts. "See, it's still warm. And I didn't buy it. I know I didn't. Somebody gave them to me. But I can't remember. Except I'm sure that it is a guy."

Katherine looked at the bag. It appeared completely normal and was, as Berry said, slightly warm to the touch. Why such a thing would send this young woman into such despair, she couldn't imagine.

"Let me take you home," Katherine suddenly felt a wave of guilty relief. She didn't need to face the fortuneteller. This young woman clearly needed her help. She could leave the carnival.

Berry shook her head vehemently. "No, no, we have to find someone."

"Who?" asked Katherine.

"I don't know," Berry admitted. "But I know it's important to find him. You see, I have this talent. I think it comes from growing up here. It's not like I'm a hero or anything, but I can find things, when I need to. That's my business. I'm a location scout for TV and movies. I find places around Cobalt City for people to film. I recently finished my first big budget commission, this huge action film, they are going to use this old mansion in Parkside for the opening sequences."

"Really? I live in that neighborhood," said Katherine. She hadn't heard of any filming, but she hadn't been paying much attention to local news recently.

"It's the old Adventurers Club. They're filming the first part of the new Solomon Cree movie there."

"And why are you at the carnival?"

"That's it. I'm not sure. We…I…the check just came through from Umberto. It's the most I've ever been paid. So I…we…came here to celebrate." She stopped and rubbed her forehead.

"You came here with someone?"

"I think I did," said Berry, "but how can I not know for sure?"

Katherine delicately shifted her sense of smell, letting the tiger inside inhale the fragrance of the young woman sitting on the bench. There was something else, a very subtle trace of somebody else, somebody masculine, lingering about her jacket. Somebody else had handled Berry's coat, and fairly recently. She could probably tell more if she leaned into the leather and gave a good snort, but she couldn't explain that to the unfortunate Berry.

"Turn out your bag," Katherine suggested. "Let's see if there is anything else in it."

Berry dumped the bag upside down on the bench, the usual litter of a busy woman's life, except for one thing. A man's leather wallet, very worn. Katherine noticed the same scent on it that she detected around the shoulders of Berry's jacket.

Berry opened it up. "There's nothing in it, just some of my business cards and some cash." She ran her fingers along the leather. "He dropped it…" she said slowly. "After he paid for the tickets. I picked it up and stuck it in my purse to keep it safe."

"Paid for what tickets?"

"The Haunted Tunnel of Love" Berry sounded definite now, more sure of herself. "I was there. Then I knew something was wrong and I had to find someone to help me. That's when I saw you."

Katherine nodded. She knew a cry for help when she heard it and she couldn't turn away. This woman needed Wild Kat.

"Stay here," she instructed Berry. "I think somebody has been playing tricks on you. It's probably nothing, but I'm going to get help. Just stay here."

"OK," said Berry, clutching her bag to her chest.

In the shadows behind the carnival booths, Katherine Wilde found an appropriately private space for a quick change. The tiger deep inside her soul stretched and let out a satisfied snarl. The hunt was on.

As always, the change from human to feline-enhanced senses took a moment of orientation. Then, costumed now as Wild Kat and with her Katherine clothes neatly rolled up and stuffed out of sight, she stepped back into the flow of the crowd.

She didn't need her heightened hearing to note the whispers and hissed comments. But this was Cobalt City, and people hung back, gave her space. A few of the more timid pretended to check their watches and then pulled their families away toward the exits. The bolder ones whipped out their digital cameras, ready to click pictures if a super-hero versus super-villain battle suddenly engulfed the place.

The carnival still swirled around her but now her sense of smell formed shapes, trails of color, like ribbons attached to each of the individuals crowding up the midway. Wild Kat stopped looking with her eyes and let her other senses take command.

Couples, pairs of ribbons entangled in their overheated pheromones, entered the Haunted Tunnel of Love. But, around the red-lit exit, the ribbons of scent broke apart, each heading in a separate direction, no longer entwined.

Wild Kat cocked her head, standing as still as a cat contemplating a mouse-hole. The dark entrance to the tunnel was empty. Too many couples had passed in and out to clearly distinguish Berry's scent, or that of her lost companion, but the feeling of something evil prickled her hair. With a low growl, Wild Kat glided forward.

Inside, the tunnel seemed larger than it appeared outside. A boat rocked upon a pool of black stagnant water. A dark figure stepped forward, an old man cloaked and hooded. "Silver for the ferryman," he croaked. "Coins, please, no paper money."

Wild Kat snarled at him and the old man shrank back.

"Couples only," he said. "No singles. She only wants couples."

"Who?" Wild Kat asked.

"Madame Prosperina."

Wild Kat looked into the tunnel. The boat seemed the only way to go forward, unless she wanted to wade through the dank water. Like any good cat, she hated getting her feet wet so she leapt lightly into the bobbing little boat.

The old man hesitated for a moment longer, then he pulled on a lever shaped like a long oar.

"You can pay me next time," he said. "Enjoy the ride."

The boat rocked and then jerked forward, gliding deeper into the tunnel. Scenes slipped past her, painted upon the fake rock walls. A young girl collecting flowers, a dark man erupting from the center of a meadow, flames shooting into the sky, an abduction into the dark earth.

The woman who lived at the center of the cat recognized classical themes. She also wondered when the "love" would replace the "haunted" in this tunnel.

The ride grew even darker. The tang of wet stone and mud, an underground smell, gave way to a strange, seductive odor, a mixture of wild thyme and catnip, of summer sunshine and winter snow, of coffee mingled with man's spicy aftershave—and then the air was clear and free of everything except a cold dusty scent, like an open empty tomb.

Wild Kat tensed. The boat rocked around a corner, gliding to a halt in a large dark pool, facing what seemed to be a cave. Behind the gauzy curtain stretched across the cave's mouth, something rustled. The tiger inside her head yowled a warning.

"Are you alone, my dear?" a woman whispered behind the curtain. "Madame Prosperina has nothing for you. Why don't you come back with your young man later? I'll tell you if his heart is true. Just a whiff of my cauldron will let you know."

The boat jerked, starting forward. Heedless of years of warnings about the dangers of standing in small boats, Wild Kat rose up and tensed her muscles. She glanced up. Pipes spewing mist ran across the ceiling.

She flung herself up, caught hold of one pipe and swung herself to the ledge running in front of the cave.

With one swipe of her claws, Wild Kat tore down the curtain to reveal a slender woman standing next to a steaming cauldron, a wand raised in one pale white hand.

"Go away!" commanded Madame Prosperina. Steam boiled out of the cauldron, a cloud of icy fragrance that drove Wild Kat back.

"Sorcery!" screamed the human part of her brain. "Prey!" prompted the tiger inside her. The strangely scented steam began to envelop her and suddenly all her senses seemed dull. She shook her head and tried to focus on the woman behind the cauldron. Her face wavered, suddenly out-of-focus, and Wild Kat felt her anger starting to drain away.

"You haven't any heart left to break. You're useless to me," said Madame Prosperina. She raised her wand again and gestured toward the door. "Go on, be a good kitty, shoo!"

"I am never a good kitty!" Wild Kat spat back, the tiger's rage overcoming the dull lassitude of Madame Prosperina's bubbling potion. She leaped over the cauldron, kicking at the wand in Madame Prosperina's hand.

The wand cracked in two. Madame Prosperina screamed as she staggered back, upsetting her cauldron so the contents spilled across the floor and drained away into the dark river flowing past her cave.

Far off, Wild Kat heard the howling of dogs, a deep baying like a hound. She could smell something else. Something old, ancient, vast. Something like Doctor Shadow, only worse.

Around them, the cave stretched, seemingly without end or hope of exit.

Years of battling the supernatural let Wild Kat close her senses to the expanding darkness around her. Instead, she grabbed Madame Prosperina's long white braid, hauling to her feet. She shook her hard, just pricking through the long black cloak with her nails.

"Don't play tricks," she said.

The sorceress snarled at her. "I married Death, why should I fear you?"

"I'm the one with claws and teeth," Wild Kat responded. "What did you do the couples who came in here?"

"I'm saving them."

"What?"

"All those foolish couples, thinking love will last forever, that they can be happy if they are only with each other. You and I, we are cleverer than that, aren't we?"

Wild Kat shook the woman again. "What are you talking about?"

"Better to forget than to be in love," said Madame Prosperina. "You should know that. I can see these things. You lost your heart long ago."

"I think you are quite mistaken. What did you do to Berry? And the others who came in here?"

"I stole their memories," confessed Madame Prosperina. "I stole their memories of each other. I made them forget the one that they were with."

"Can you restore them?"

With a grimace, the sorceress pointed at her shattered wand and upset cauldron. "The spell is already broken. They will go back to being the same foolish, lovestruck idiots that they were." She pulled away from Wild Kat and wrapped her cloak more firmly around herself. The sorceress began to sink into the ground, melting away like a certain Wicked Witch. As she disappeared, she made one last mocking comment, "Go ask the fortuneteller for one of his slips of paper. He knows what happened to your heart."

Then the cave was only an empty alcove, built out of canvas and metal piping. Wild Kat looked over her shoulder. A boat glided into the pool carrying a young couple. The woman screamed when she saw Wild Kat crouched at the edge of the now tiny pond. Her date pulled her tight into his embrace. "It's only a wax dummy," he said to the girl and kissed her soundly. The girl giggled. The boat jerked and passed through a curtain.

An empty boat slid past. Wild Kat jumped onboard. It carried her out of the Haunted Tunnel of Love and back into the garishly lit midway of the carnival.

She made her way back to the bench where she had left the distraught redhead, but Berry didn't need her any more. A stocky young man was sitting next to the redhead, clutching both her hands tightly in his.

"It was so weird," he said to Berry. "I was halfway home when I realized that I'd left you at the carnival. So I turned around and came right back. We need a break, babe, we've both been working way too hard. How could I forget and leave you here?"

"It is OK now," said Berry. "You found me." She snuggled closer to him, resting her head on his shoulder.

Wild Kat smiled and turned away. All around her, couples were joining up again, with glad cries and quick kisses, hugs and exclamations.

Then she spotted it, the sideshow tent with the poster advertising Unfortunate John the Two-faced Oracle.

Forgetting that she still was Wild Kat and not Katherine, she stepped through the entrance. Once again, she faced a nondescript little man seated behind a plain table. But there was a scent lingering in the air, a scent of something ancient and powerful. Something like what she'd smelled in Madame Prosperina's cave but different also.

He looked up at her and then pushed the clay bowl full of strips of paper towards her. "Pick one," he said, "and I will tell you your past."

"I don't care about my past," snarled Wild Kat, leaning on the table with her claws out. She scratched long furrows into the wood.

"You should," he said. "Knowing your past can change your future."

"Your fortune killed Claudine!"

"Did it?" said Unfortunate John. "Or did it show her a fate that she lacked the will to change? Did your fortune kill you?"

"*Omnia causa fiunt*," said a second voice from the back of the tent. Once again Wild Kat saw shadows crawling up the walls, the shadow of a man with two faces.

"Indeed," said Unfortunate John, "all things happen for a reason. Like old gods trapped in a carnival or a young girl seeing her future written on a slip of paper."

"How can you stand it?" she asked him. "To ruin people's lives like that."

"I don't do anything. I give them a glimpse of their future and their past. If they are wise, they learn from what I tell them. If not, then what can I do? I'm just a sideshow freak trapped in a carnival," he replied. "That's why they call me Unfortunate John, even though I would prefer them to call me Janus. Now, do you want to draw again and learn your past? Or are you done?"

"Madame Prosperina dared me to do it."

"Another relic of another era," shrugged the little man. "And far angrier about her fate than me. Go on, draw one. You're strong enough to face backwards."

She stretched out her hand and snagged one slip of paper on the tip of a claw. As she opened it, Unfortunate John's second voice stated: "*Abstulit qui dedit.*"

It had been too many years since she studied Latin. She looked to the little man for translation.

"He who gave it, took it," he said.

"What?"

"Once you held a man's heart, his love, and when he left, he took your heart with him."

She shook her head. "No. There's never been anyone like that. Not in my past."

The little man shrugged. "Only you can truly interpret the phrase. But I can tell you this. Until you understand it, your heart will remain frozen. That much I can see clearly."

Suddenly all Wild Kat wanted was to find her clothes. Like her teenage self, she longed to flee the carnival. However she didn't throw away the paper fortune crumpled in her hand. Instead she carefully tucked it inside her costume, next to her heart, to contemplate another day.

"I am finished with your games," she told Unfortunate John.

He nodded and then cocked his head to one side, as if someone or something just whispered in his ear. "Unusual," he said. "But fair enough. You can draw once more."

"What?"

"Draw again, one more slip. For the city's fortune this time. Apparently you are the keeper of its doorways as much as I was when I once held Rome in my protection."

"You are a very strange man," she said.

"No," he answered, "I am one old and very tired god. Draw and let me finish this night."

Some compulsion pushed her hand forward and she drew out a final strip of paper. This one was black with white writing running across it.

"Ah," said Unfortunate John, "one of those."

"*Novus ordo seclorum,*" his second voice said.

"A new order for the ages," he translated.

"And what does it mean?" But even as she asked, she felt the answer blossoming inside her. "Are changes coming to Cobalt City?"

"Old heroes will fall," he said.

"But, we can shape our futures. You said so."

Unfortunate John nodded at her.

"Then, no matter how many heroes fall," said Wild Kat, clutching the fortune tightly in her hand and feeling a sudden unreasonable but undeniable lightness in her heart, "new ones will rise. Because this is Cobalt City!"

She left Unfortunate John to his dark little tent and his bowl of obscure phrases. The world was changing, Wild Kat could feel it as surely as the tiger roaring in her soul. But she could face her past, and she could confront her future. All the choices in the world were hers to make.

Soon, the carnival would pull up stakes and leave. But the city, her beloved Cobalt City, would endure. She carried that certain knowledge with her into the night.

Rosemary Jones writes. Some days she writes about super-heroes in Cobalt City, some days she writes adventures set in the Forgotten Realms, and some days she writes other stuff. When she's not writing, she's reading, including back issues of Tigra, Sheena, and Rima the Jungle Girl. You can check out all her latest forays into fiction at www.rosemaryjones.com.

A Snowflake's Chance in Hell
Jeremy Zimmerman

(*Warning: Contains Snowflake*)

I can't think of a more undignified place for a hyper-evolved panda to die than a portable toilet. But there I was, overheating in a box filled with the smell of shit and that sickly sweet, fruit-scented crap they put in there. My only hope lay in the cell phone clutched in my furry hand. "Pick up!"

"What do you want, Snowflake?" Kara Sparx said when she finally picked up the phone.

"Kara, where have you been?" I screamed. "We have an emergency here!"

"Snowflake, calm down. What's the emergency?"

"You know the hologram projector you made for me? The one that makes me look human? Someone stole it!"

She sighed. "You mean the one-of-a-kind prototype?"

That statement caused my gut to twist up and a deeper element of panic seeped in. I squeaked, "Yes."

"Okay, chill. It's not a big deal. I can probably make you another one in about a week."

"A week? What am I supposed to do for a week? I'm trapped in a portable toilet, dying of heat stroke or something!" On cue, someone tugged at the locked door. "Occupied, asshole! Look, Kara, pandas don't sweat. This is really life threatening. I was not genetically engineered to hide in an incubator filled with shit."

"Look, I'm sorry. My home has been invaded by a pint-sized force of chaos. I can't really spend time in my lab."

I pounded my fist on the plastic wall in frustration. "Then get Doctor Shadow to purge the chaos and come to the carnival to help me find it. I can't go outside like this. The world isn't ready for this much fuzzy."

"The chaos is actually my niece, and I'm trying to keep her and my sister away from the cape and cowl set. What the hell are you doing at the carnival? Did you not get the memo? It's a bad place!"

I rested my head against the door in defeat. "Yeah, I got the memo."

"Then why are you there?"

"They have these polish sausages on a stick I couldn't resist. They smother them in this thick barbeque sauce, and it's just...wonderful."

"Oh, for the love of...I need to get back to work. You need to panda up and just figure out your own solution—"

"Hey, pandas are shy and gentle animals. Like me."

"Fine, then man up. You're in the middle of a carnival. People will just think you're in a costume. Then just walk out and bum a ride off someone from the Protectorate. I hear Huntsman is working on a learner's permit."

And then she hung up on me.

I pounded my head against the wall a few times. I had to stop when I realized that it was rocking the whole Port-a-Poo box. The last thing I needed was to have the whole thing tip over and cover me in other people's waste.

After a failed attempt at deep cleansing breaths to calm my nerves, followed by a few moments fighting back the gag reflex, I opened the door and stumbled out into the summer sunlight. A few people glanced my way, but only children paid me much attention. My mission to rescue my disguise was thwarted by a swarm of tiny children hugging my legs and nearly headbutting my junk.

Have I mentioned I hate kids?

It took me an hour to escape the rugrats. Every damn brat wanted to have a picture taken with me. Even after I left the carnival I still got stopped every ten feet by some snot-nosed runt who wanted a photo op. Finally, I broke down and bought some weird carnival mask with a big hooked nose and covered in red and black squares. I don't think it went with my Hawaiian shirt, but it freaked out the kids enough that they didn't come near me. And then I went hunting for my hologram projector.

I hadn't seen who had nabbed it, so I wandered through the carnival and stared hard at every person who looked remotely weird. Unfortunately for me, there were a lot of weird-looking people. Some of them even worked for the carnival.

Luck proved to be on my side, though, when I caught a glimpse of my illusionary human form. I knew that face almost as well as I knew my own, and it was sitting on a bench and seemed to be people watching. It was weird to look at the hologram from the outside.

I felt underwhelmed by the lack of villainy. This guy stole my most valuable personal possession, and all he used it for was people watching?

He didn't seem to see me, so I angled my path to pass behind him on the bench, then I laid my hand on his shoulder and said, "I think you have something of mine."

As my hand passed through the hologram, I realized that I wasn't touching a flesh and blood shoulder. Instead, it felt cold and wooden. And it moved freely when I touched it. I grabbed hold and pulled it towards me. I held some sort of weird Russian nesting doll. The babushka on it looked cute and grandmotherly until it split along the seam to reveal several rows of teeth.

Leave it to me to make enemies with evil *tchotchkes*.

The little bastard bit me. I screamed in pain and dropped the thing as I ran backwards. On the ground, it split open and disgorged its nested contents, which all came at me with toothy maws. As I freaked out and fled from the bitey Russian dolls, it set off a chain reaction of panic around me.

Not wanting to lose my target, I looked back towards the bench in time to see the hologram dissolve, revealing a capuchin monkey surrounded by small piles of cheap toys. Some of them looked pretty old. The projector had fallen onto the ground in front of the bench. The monkey held a fluid-filled jar with something pale floating in it. Clinging onto the monkey's back was what looked like a mummified two-headed baby. With the illusion gone, the toys all scattered and fled into the crowd.

The monkey clambered up to the top of one of the tents, still carrying the mummy baby and the weird jar. Hanging around the monkey's neck was my hologram projector. I moved to chase after it, but fell after a stinging pain in my ankles. The sight of my hologram projector had caused me to forget the stupid Russian dolls, which now swarmed over my legs, biting me.

I crawled forward, trying to kick and bat away the biting things. People ran in confusion in all directions, occasionally trampling over me. Ahead, I spotted my salvation: A "Test Your Strength" booth. Fueled by a surge of hope, I pulled myself up and staggered toward the booth.

I grabbed the hammer from where the booth operator had left it propped against the Hi-Striker, shook loose one of the dolls gnawing on my leg and then backed up to swing my hammer down. The *tchotchke* shattered with a cloud of orange smoke and the smell of sulfur. I crowed with laughter and began knocking other ones off to smash. Soon, I was free of the buggers.

With my legs covered in stinging bite marks, I limped off through the carnival in search of that damn dirty ape. Or monkey. Whatever.

After twenty minutes of wandering around looking for that stupid critter, I caught a glimpse of him scampering through a window into the "Museum of the Strange." On one side of the door was a suit of medieval armor that had too many arms. On the other, a statue of the Buddha holding a bundle of cigars.

I stared in confusion for a moment at the Buddha until something clicked. "Right. Cigar store Indian. Someone's going to have to die for that."

Flipping off the Buddha as I went inside, I handed my ticket to the pizza-faced kid at the door and moved into the exhibit. The smell of formaldehyde and dust nearly overwhelmed me. Tall glass-fronted shelves filled the area, while the narrow walkway formed a maze. Hushed conversation and laughter came from other parts of the building.

Each shelf was filled with gewgaws, weird artifacts from the far corners of the world and dead things in jars. Every item had a notecard with a handwritten description in cramped letters. One shelf had a feral Kewpie doll in a cage, pacing back and forth. Another said it was the flaming sword of Manjushri. I couldn't figure out how they kept it burning in the case. A third held a jar with a dead baby unicorn floating in brine.

At a wide spot in the exhibit, a dark frame hung in front of an upright arcade machine. A sign next to it read, "Gaze into the Mirror of Shadows! See your darkest self! Only 25 cents!"

I'd heard the Protectorate talk about the Mirror of Shadows. They never told me what it did, but I was pretty certain it was secure in some place that wasn't the Creepy Carnival. Overcome by curiosity, I set my mallet next to the machine, put my two bits into the slot and waited while lights played across the surface of the mirror.

After a moment, the mirror showed me an image of something that looked more like a mix of panda bear and grizzly. It stood hunched over, with thick cords of muscle visible through its dense, spiky fur. The creature's brow was furrowed, as though it was perpetually scowling, and its teeth looked more carnivore-oriented than mine.

All in all, I looked pretty badass. I wondered if I could get some genetic upgrades like that. I flexed my biceps in different directions and saw my doppelganger match my motion.

A bell chimed and a card dropped out of a slot in the bottom half of the machine. I picked it up and saw that it said, "You have now been tainted by the Mirror of Shadows. Redeem this card for a free small ice cream in the Treat Pavilion." Today was picking up.

As I pocketed the card, a frail male voice said next to me, "Can I help you?"

I jolted in alarm, but refrained from screaming. Mostly. I turned to see a thin old man in a dark suit, hunched over as though he was too thin to support his weight. Sharp chin, sharp nose, and a thin fringe of hair around his otherwise bald head left me feeling like I'd seen him in a cartoon somewhere.

On the man's shoulder sat the monkey, the hologram projector still hanging from its neck. I screamed, staggered backwards and fumbled for my mallet, knocking it over in the process. I knelt and patted around me to find the handle of my weapon, not willing to take my eyes off the old man and his little thief.

"Yeah, you can help me by giving my back the bracelet that little fleabag has stolen."

"I believe you're mistaken." The old man patted the monkey affectionately. "Not only does little Miko not have any fleas, but his bracelet was a gift given to him by an Egyptian princess."

"Wait a second! Kara isn't either Egyptian or a princess. At least, not that I know of." Still no sign of the mallet. I fought hard not to look down.

He looked around the room, then shook his head. "I do not know who this Kara is, but that is not where we received this bracelet."

My fingers found the handle of my mallet, and I slowly picked it up. "Fine, but Egypt doesn't have any princesses."

"Actually, they do. But this was not the currently living one. Our Egyptian princess has been living a state of undeath for some time."

"Then ask this undead princess where she got the bracelet," I growled.

"I'm afraid the mummification process has quite destroyed her ability to speak. But I find I do not care where the bracelet originated. It allows Miko and his little friends a degree of freedom to travel through the carnival, and I do not have the heart to let a panda in a carnival mask take that freedom away from them."

"Then I'll just have to take it back, Mr. Spooky-Pants," I said as I raised my mallet and charged.

My mallet hit the ground on the far side, passing through him harmlessly. The momentum pulled me through the intangible form of the coot, which left me feeling cold and filled my mouth with the taste of ashes. Like kissing a smoker, or Mister Grey, just a hundred times worse.

While I spat to get the taste out of my mouth, the monkey jumped onto my back. Soon my head was a mass of pain from the thing clawing and biting. I ran uncontrollably, scrambling to get a grip on the little bastard. Glass shattered as I broke some of the display cases open with my flailing.

I may have also screamed. Just a little.

After an eternity of biting and clawing, I pulled the curtain climber off and threw him to the ground. The monkey scampered back to its master and up onto the creepster's back. A noise from behind drew my attention and I saw a handful of people staring. I guess the noise had attracted the other museum patrons.

"Now, look what you've done," the old man said. He shook his head wearily. "All this mess. All these witnesses. Your disappearances are going to cause quite the stir, and the head of the carnival will have to chide me. But what can be done?"

I tried to ask what he was talking about, but my mouth no longer wanted to form words. The room grew dark around me, and soon I felt the impact of my face on the floor as darkness completely descended.

When I woke up again, I found myself upright but unable to move. I looked down to see that some sort of thick spider web pinned me to a wall. All around me were the other people I had seen before blacking out, similarly trapped. Some freckle-faced kid, maybe ten years old, was hanging on the wall opposite, staring at me.

While I struggled with the web, the kid asked, "Are you really a panda?"

I paused, breathless from my brief struggle, and said, "Yes."

"I hear pandas don't know how to have sex. Is that true?"

I glared at the runt. "That's not what your mom said last night."

The kid looked over at the woman next to him in confusion.

She worked her jaw in alarm.

"Mom?"

"Billy," she said, once she found her ability to speak again. "Don't listen to anything that filthy animal says to you."

Oops.

I focused my attention back on my bonds. I've played enough video games to know that webs are flammable. I looked around at the other captives and called out, "Does anyone here smoke?"

Everyone shook their heads except one little old lady who harrumphed and said, "I don't think is the time to be worrying about cigarettes."

"No, I want to try and burn the web. If there's someone who smokes here, they might be able to burn away the webbing and then free the rest of us."

"Ah, well let me see what I can do. I keep it in my brassiere, but I might be able to reach it. I used to be quite flexible in my day."

"Great!" I shouted, trying to contain my grimace.

After a few minutes, the web disappeared with a whoomp and the old broad fell to the ground face-first. Then she didn't move.

"Oh my god," someone said. "You killed her!"

Shouts of alarm filled the room. If they hadn't all been pinned to the walls, I might have been lynched right there.

126

Luckily for all of us, she soon roused and slowly stood up while dusting off her floral print dress.

"Woo-wee," she said. "Knocked the wind right out of me. Who wants out next?"

Everyone, including me, began to shout, "Me! Me! Me!" The old woman shrugged at the cacophony and began melting the webbing off of the people nearest her. I was the third one freed, and I gave the old dame a huge hug.

"Thank you so much. I'll be sure my bosses at the Protectorate get you a reward of some kind." Everyone ooooh-ed when they heard I worked for the Protectorate. I paused a moment to let them stare at me with rightful awe before saying to the old woman, "What's your name?"

"Ethel," she said. "Ethel Schneider. You?"

"Snowflake," I said.

"Snowflake's a gay name," said Billy from the wall.

"Billy!" his mother yelled.

"Not that there's anything wrong with being gay," he added sullenly.

"Can we let him down last?" I asked.

Once we were all free, with Billy sobbing as he realized I meant it for him to be last, I led the group through the back rooms of the museum. More web-covered bodies were trapped back here, some smaller than others. We tried freeing them, but found that the people that were trapped in them had become vegetables. I mean that metaphorically, mostly. Well, some of them looked a little like veggies when we opened the spider silk wrapping.

See, other cocoons held similar trinkets and gewgaws like the ones that fled the hologram earlier. Plus there were the occasional heads of broccoli or whatever. The objects twitched feebly when freed from their confinement, but then stopped moving. I wondered how many of those *tchotchkes* had once been captured carnival patrons.

The museum seemed much larger than its outside appearance, but soon we found a door back into the museum proper and made it outside. Night had long since fallen and the carnival was silent around us. We hurried towards the exit, but my departure was slowed by the sight of a small form running along the top of one of the ramshackle buildings.

I abandoned the rest of the group and ran towards the monkey. I managed to catch up near the Ferris wheel.

"Miko," I growled.

Miko shrieked back at me.

I moved to climb up the side of the building he was on, but he threw the hologram bracelet over my head and ran off in the other direction. I jumped to catch it, felt it brush my extended fingertip and then it hit the ground with a sickening crack and fizzle sound. I didn't need to worry about finding it in the dark. My disguise as a middle-aged Caucasian was clearly visible, though it was doing some sort of cha-cha dance rather than responding to biometric cues.

With a heavy heart, I picked up the bracelet and walked back towards the exit. The hologram shorted out halfway there, so I wasn't followed by the dancing man anymore. Ethel waited in the parking lot. Only my car and one that I assumed was hers still remained.

"Wow, you waited for me?" I asked. It was nice to know that after all this crap, someone still cared about me.

"I wasn't going to let a reward from the Protectorate slip through my fingers," she said. My faith in humanity dropped a notch. "Think I could meet any of them? My favorite is Stardust. He has a cute tush when he's not wearing that armor."

Jeremy Zimmerman lives in Seattle, with his wife and five bossy cats. A County bureaucrat by day, he turns to his writing as an outlet for the stories and voices in his head. After writing for game companies, he has shifted his focus to fiction. His prose can be found in *Crossed Genre Magazine*, Wily Writers Podcast, *10Flash Quarterly* and other anthologies by Timid Pirate Publishing. Visit his website at http://www.bolthy.com for more info.

Carnival Heart
de Bie, Jones Vogel, J. Zimmerman

The carnival had been in Cobalt for a week, its true psychic cost to the city ratcheting up invisibly with each day that went by. Not that estimating damages made any sense at this point. Like a tornado in tarpaulin, it would spin and wheel and only once it was gone could a reliable headcount be made. Despite a city of heroes, despite over a century of visits to Cobalt, not one of them truly understood what the Carnaval Pomme D'or was. Not even Dr. Shadow and his several thousand years of accumulated magical knowledge saw the beast nested within the carnival's heart.

But I knew. Yes, I, the lowly occultist Louis Malenfant, had insight the city's protectors could never dream of. Or rather the King in Yellow had the insight. And tethered to him like an anchor in the mud of this world, I knew what others did not. Madness, it would seem, had its privileges. I saw his plan, the pieces he had moved into place. And I saw my part in this venture. Though I tried to deny it, my patron's will cannot be bent by the likes of me. But first, I must collect the others, the King tells me.

--- From the burned journal found in Lafayette Park

Wild Kat decided to take the north exit out of the carnival. From there, it would be a short walk to the deli to restock the freezer. She was out of double chocolate chip mint and, after her trip through the Haunted Tunnel of Love and her encounter with Unfortunate John, she knew she needed a pint. Probably more.

The uncomfortably familiar sight of Louis Malenfant in the archway leading from the fairgrounds blocked her path. She suppressed a shudder at the subtle wrongness he evoked, like a tumor floating in the world's punch bowl. "You are needed."

"Not now," she snarled, trying to push past him. "I have had a day!"

"I know how to make the Carnaval Pomme D'or hurt. I thought you may want to get in on that."

She paused, turning back to watch the spinning lights of the Ferris wheel. Far off in the distance, she could hear the music still spilling out of the Haunted Tunnel of Love, and the laughter of happy couples.

"Can we shut this place down?" she asked Malenfant.

His eyes sparkled madly. "Perhaps. Their stay here is almost up anyway. But with your help we might be able to encourage them not to return. For how long," he smiled, "it depends on how hard we hit them. I can't do this alone. My…patron…he will be of no direct help here."

A child shoved past them and approached a stocky man in a hooded sweatshirt and handed over an armload of cotton candy and caramel apples.

"Thanks, kid," the man said in a familiar voice. An ursine scent overrode the sticky sweet smell of carnival treats.

"Snowflake!" Wild Kat yelled. The man looked up, revealing a panda face in the shadows of the hood. Snowflake waved at them. He looked a little guilty.

"Um, hello!" Snowflake swallowed nervously. "What's shaking?"

"We need to talk," Malenfant gestured at them. "Away from here. Away from where the carnival can hear us."

Snowflake's eyes widened. "The carnival can hear us?"

Wild Kat looked back at the shadows growing behind the glowing lights of the sideshows and rides. "Perhaps it can! Let's get out of here."

Once they gained some distance from the gate, Snowflake asked with his cheeks bulging like a chipmunk, "So what's all the hubbub, bub?"

Malenfant ignored him, turning to Wild Kat. "My patron tells me that you have in your possession a weaponized cutting laser. I suggest you bring it. We shall need it."

"The cutting laser? Why didn't you say this involved the cutting laser? I'm totally in if I get to use that baby again!" Snowflake interjected.

Louis Malenfant fixed him with a thin smile. "I need you to do something first. Bring Kara and her companion back with you."

"That weird robot?" Snowflake sighed. "He's nothing but trouble, pal."

"That's what we need. Explosions, distractions, confusions, and combustion."

Wild Kat smiled grimly. "I know someone else ideal for such a mission. I'll contact him. Where do you want to meet?"

"Schrodinger's Cup," the unsettling occultist said. "Noon tomorrow."

Wild Kat nodded. She knew the place well. "Tomorrow is the last day of the carnival. Why wait?"

Louis Malenfant smiled, his thin lips pulled taught over too-white teeth. "Because tomorrow the carnival will be sated, slow, and unprepared for resistance."

Wild Kat didn't like waiting. But that smile made her itch. She decided it best not to argue with the man coming to them with a plan. Her claws retracted and her fingers flew as she texted Stardust where and when to meet them.

Malenfant sipped on his milk tea in the corner table of Schrodinger's Cup. He eyed the assembled heroes. They eyed him back with various expressions of distrust—except for the ever cheerful Stardust. He seemed to be busy admiring the reflection of his holographic disguise in the mirror hanging behind the table. Or perhaps he was admiring the reflections of the people in the room. Louis never understood other people, especially well-adjusted ones.

"Well, we are here," Wild Kat said. "What do you want?"

Setting down his cup, Louis Malenfant tapped his fingertips together like a university professor ready to explain quantum mechanics to toddlers. "Here is the fundamental difference between the King in Yellow and a God. A God has a sense of identity. They are someone or something foolish enough to fence off part of a concept and pretend that they own it. The King in Yellow just is. Like the carnival."

The coffee-jockey from behind the counter came and cleared the table next to them, eyeing the hologram-disguised panda suspiciously. It was clear that he recognized inventor and industrialist Jaccob Stevens because of his well-known public identity of Stardust. But Malenfant's mood and lack of reflection in the wall mirror mounted behind him compelled the teenager not to linger.

Once the barista was done wiping down the table, Malenfant continued. "Most people have made the mistake in thinking that the carnival is run by magic, or powered by magic. They are wrong. The practitioners of magic who call the Carnaval Pomme D'or home are merely moths to the flame," he shook his head, unhappy with the metaphor, "No, no, more like mushrooms on a tree or sucker fish on the side of a whale. The Carnaval Pomme D'or is an entity, roaming around the coil, though mostly on this world. Before it was a carnival, it was a gypsy camp, before that, something else entirely. It has been among us for a long time, hidden beneath the parasites that have attached themselves to it. And some of those parasites have been attached for centuries, getting fat on the blood that the carnival attracts to it in every new town."

"So, how do we make it leave Cobalt City?" asked Stardust.

"And never come back," added Wild Kat.

"The problem thus far has been that you cape-and-cowl types have thought of the carnival as a place, or a collective, and have dealt with it as such. A fortune teller here, or midway malcontent there. All you have done is pluck the parasites from the real menace. We need to strike not only at the dangerous distractions crawling on the surface, but also at the heart of the carnival itself." Malenfant leaned forward. "That is where the laser comes in…"

While Stardust did aerial recon, Wild Kat crouched in the shadows cast by fun cars in the end of the kiddie ride alley. Everything seemed good down here, as though the carnival had no idea what was coming. She tapped her earpiece. "What are you seeing?"

"Nothing to report," Stardust said. "It looks really quiet up here, actually…woah. Dragon."

"Dragon?" Wild Kat said.

"Uh, yeah. Just a second."

She had to pull the earpiece out when a cacophony of roars and the z-zap! of Stardust's gauntlet blasters tore through her head. She heard the telltale sound of billowing flame and metal crashing into unforgiving earth, which then turned into feedback. It left her dazed for a second.

"Jaccob?" Kat put the earpiece back in. "Jaccob!!"

A voice garbled through the static. "Well, we seem to have got their attention now."

Wild Kat visualized the crash, the golden bolts from Stardust's bracers. She was glad she had recruited Knockabout and Gallows to evacuate potential civilian casualties, essentially snatching them with an apology on the other end of their unexpected teleportation. Now Stardust could cut loose without too much concern. "You got the dragon?"

"Totally disintegrated. Yeah…no, we're good. We're good. Oww."

Wild Kat had a suspicion. "Was that you, Lumien?"

"Your question is unclear," the robot said. "Please specify."

"Did you use a holographic dragon to make Stardust crash into something?"

The robot considered. "Maybe."

133

The earpiece buzzed as Stardust took to the air again to survey the situation. "Wild Kat, we've got a problem."

"What's going on?" Her claws extended almost with her noticing. She sniffed the air, trying to pick up some trace of the threat. Sun-baked canvas, dust, carnival foods, the lingering tang of bile near the tilt-a-whirl, but nothing that signaled a direct threat. "I'm not seeing anything down on the ground."

"They're close to the ground, to the north of your locations. My sensors are picking up about a hundred small bogeys at thirty feet out and closing."

"I don't see anything…wait. How small?"

A wave of puppets swarmed over her position from the cover of the miniature cars with the clack of tiny wooden feet as they clambered across the fiberglass hoods. Wild Kat weaved and dodged, slashing with her claws, but the puppets kept coming. When she ripped the head off one evil Punch, his Judy just grabbed it and smacked it back on her man. Wild Kat realized quickly that her normal fighting methods weren't going to work here.

Wild Kat sprang over the fun cars, vaulting over the thin iron railing and onto the roof of the ticket booth. A few dozen puppets tumbled into the mini Aston Martin and started it. The car sprang off the track and drove across the plastic flowers, tiny houses, and cardboard Matterhorn. They plowed over the Swiss Miss and her small brown cow, knocking down the white fence and the "you must be this tall" sign.

The car rammed into the ticket booth, shaking it more severely than Wild Kat would have liked. If not for super-human reflexes, she might not have kept her balance on the roof. "Shit," she muttered.

"What?" Stardust's voice over the earpiece sounded surprised. "Did you just swear?"

"I have a bunch of crazed puppets driving a tiny red convertible trying to run me down."

Stardust went silent for a few seconds. "Puppets?"

"Primarily marionettes," she reported, "but there are a few Indonesian shadow puppets of the Wayang Kulit persuasion in the mix as well."

"No ventriloquist dummies, though?" said Stardust.

"The night's still young," she smiled despite herself and the repeated shaking of the ticket booth. She wasn't sure how long it would hold up under this abuse, and the little wooden menaces were starting to climb. "Anyway, evil to fight. We'll chat later." Wild Kat eyed the distance between the roof of the ticket booth and the top of the merry-go-round. She crouched down and then made the leap, stretching out her claws to grab the roof of the carousel, landing with a thump above the painted wooden horses.

"Oh yeah, baby! Who needs jets in their boots!" she pumped her fist in the air at the spiraling figure of Stardust above.

The puppets swung their tiny car around, dozens of manic figures clinging to the sides like a bus in India. Several dozen more flowed after them like a choppy wake of cloth and wood as they raced up the midway after her. Wild Kat swung off the roof of the merry-go-round and sprinted toward the bubbly sugar smell of the caramel apple concession. She sprung through the open window of the stand and landed behind the counter. She grabbed the pot of sticky, bubbling goo used to coat the apples.

Wild Kat jumped out of the window of the concession stand and moved to the middle of the path. The puppets raced toward her. She smiled, raising the pot of caramel above her head. With a battle cry of "Eat sugar, Pinocchio!" she tossed the pot over the lot over as many as she could candy-coat.

The blinded puppets, stuck to their racing vehicle, careened past her and smashed into the popcorn booth. It had confounded the fastest of her pursuit, but the click-clack sound of the puppet mob that followed behind the vanguard assured her there was still ample trouble coming.

"I could use a little heat down here!" Wild Kat radioed to Stardust.

"Happy to oblige!" he chortled. A wide golden blast of his signature starbolts sprang from Stardust's gauntlets and engulfed the sugary puppets. Those that avoided the air assault broke ranks and ran. The smell of burnt wood and toasted caramel filled the air.

Like a huge, brass engine of death, Lumien careened into the midway, stomping the scattering puppets as though he had a vendetta against them. With deadly efficiency, he stomped and lunged, throwing holographic illusions of flame to herd the stragglers his way. Wild Kat had to admit, she was glad he was on their side.

"Nice!" said Wild Kat.

"Uh oh," said Stardust's voice in her ear.

"What's the problem?" she asked.

"Ferris wheel."

"Seriously?" She looked across the tents in Stardust's direction and saw the furiously spinning Ferris wheel lift from the carnival grounds.

"Well, at least it's not a dragon," Stardust announced, always happy to find the silver-lining in a situation. At that moment, the Ferris wheel's spinning cars ignited and threw a ball of fire towards the armored hero. Wild Kat heard only the muted ghost of an obscenity as her friend and team member was briefly engulfed in flames.

Snowflake, Kara, and Malenfant stood in front of a nondescript tent while Stardust's jets roared above them. There was no sign on the threadbare canvas, a faded red that could have been hundreds of years old. Musty bales of hay were piled along the sides, and a sharp reek of animal urine pervaded the air. "Well, I guess I can understand why no one would give this place a second look," Kara said, trying not to breathe.

"So that's it? We just go in there and laser something, right?" Snowflake asked. "And does the smell get any better?"

"In time," Malenfant said. "We must pierce through its shell to attack the entity within. The carnival will, of course, send protectors to fend us off."

As if on cue, a pale-haired woman stepped through the tent flaps, wearing a bedazzled bikini and a knife harness.

"Sateen, the Razor Dancer," Malenfant whispered.

Snowflake stood up straighter. "Well, hello. Will there be wrestling?"

"I don't think you bring knives to a wrestling match," Kara whispered, slipping her zap guns from their holsters. She fired two quick blasts from each and was disappointed to see the knife thrower neatly anticipate her aim, with all four shots missing by inches. Rethinking her strategy, Kara shifted behind Snowflake. Malenfant similarly moved behind the panda's bulky form.

Snowflake craned his neck around to look at Kara. "Where did you learn to shoot? Stormtrooper Academy?" His attention was drawn back to the knife dancer when he heard the sound of knives being drawn. Sateen stood with a knife in each hand, mouth opened to reveal a smile filled with hundreds of silvered, needle-sharp teeth. Eyes sparkling, she charged the panda.

"You seem a little less sexy all of a sudden," Snowflake said as he backpedaled away. He bumped into Malenfant and the two of them fell over.

Kara fired up her jet pack and flew up from behind Snowflake, zap guns at the ready as she waited to take her shot. Sateen, focused on Snowflake, could not evade Kara's first shot and grunted as it hit. But it was not enough to stop the knife thrower, and the second shot ricocheted off one of the blades. Kara veered abruptly to the right, dodging out of the way of a thrown knife.

Snowflake blindly fired his laser, screaming as he cut a jagged arc through the top of the tent, missing Sateen entirely. After a few seconds, he released the trigger and stopped screaming. He and Sateen both looked up to see part of the tent roof collapse inward while the edges smoldered. Then she turned

137

and looked back at the panda with a cruel smile. Already, the carnival was healing itself, and the tent's canvas started to regrow across the burned hole.

Sateen's poise was broken as Kara's feet planted between her shoulder blades, knocking the Razor Dancer forward. Kara tried to drive the other woman fully to the ground, but Sateen writhed and contorted to strike Kara in the foot with a long, glittering blade. Kara flew up and back, the knife protruding from the tip of her boot. She fired both zap guns as she went, a bit of blind panic in her eyes. The knife thrower dodged one sizzling blast, but was struck by the second in the face. She flew backwards in a daze.

As Sateen lay there stunned, Snowflake scrambled to his feet and pinned the knife fighter by throwing his furry torso across hers. "Someone tie her up before she shivs me?"

"I've got some zip ties here," Kara called out as she reached into her pocket.

A muffled scream and violent thrashing drew their attention back towards their captive. Her arms and legs slapped and twitched beneath Snowflake's body, pounding hard against the tramped down carnival grounds. Bloody foam flecked her lips in full grand mal seizure. Snowflake climbed off of the knife thrower with wide eyes. A symbol had been written on her forehead with black magic marker, the skin around it erupting in a spiderweb of blackened veins. Malenfant knelt next to her, an uncapped marker in his hand. "We should move. She'll be quite angry if she manages to return from the place I just sent her spirit. But, she should have never escaped from there to begin with." He looked at the knife still sticking from Kara's boot. "You're hurt?"

"Steel-toed boots," she said, distracted as she looked at the knife thrower's body. "The tip barely nicked me."

Snowflake couldn't take his narrowed eyes off of Louis Malenfant. "Dude, what kind of super-hero are you?" Snowflake asked.

Malenfant shrugged. "Who said I was a hero?"

Kara had mentioned the killer Ferris wheel in the pre-mission brief at Schrodinger's Cup, so Stardust wasn't entirely surprised when it pulled free of its supports with a groan and started spinning like a buzz saw. Then it lit on fire, as though each of the cars was a Molotov cocktail. Seeing as Kara had not mentioned the firestorm angle, Stardust thought that maybe the Carnaval Pomme D'or had made some upgrades.

Even as the fire exploded over him, Stardust swerved to avoid being forced to the ground again. Too many things down there to catch fire, and recent property damage workshops were fresh in his mind. His suit's force screen kept the worst of the flames away, but some managed so bleed through. It burned at his armor in exactly the way fire isn't supposed to burn metal. The flames clung to him and nipped at his suit like a swarm of piranhas. Fire piranhas.

"Stupid magic!" Stardust said as he jetted higher into the sky. The Ferris wheel followed, undulating as it flew to throw balls of flame after its quarry.

At least the plan was working. Stardust wasn't entirely clear on why, when Malenfant had asked for a volunteer to generate the distraction, everyone had pointed at him. There was only so subtle a guy could be when his shiny armor trailed a golden nimbus everywhere he went, but he wasn't entirely without subtlety.

The Ferris wheel didn't seem to have a problem with altitude and followed him up through the clouds. The thinner air diminished its fires, however, which was a good sign. At least it didn't completely break the laws of science.

"I was meaning to use this on the dragon or at least where everyone could see it," Stardust said to the Ferris wheel. "But you...you defy the laws of physics so much that it makes me tired."

He righted himself and reversed course, flying straight toward the wheel. It spun crazily and hurled a particularly large ball of flame, which he dodged. Stardust raised his hands, channeled power into a special device he'd crafted just for today, and cut loose.

A shockwave of sound burst from Stardust's hands as he flew, shaking the metal bones of the Ferris wheel. The sound waves smothered the flames in an instant, leaving only a charred wreck floating in the atmosphere just before Stardust smashed into it. He bore it back down the mile or so to earth. His internal sensors indicated he was on target to hit the middle of the carnival, right about where the wheel had been spinning only minutes before.

"Heads up, folks! Big wheel coming in for a bigger boom," Stardust said.

He liked big booms. He just hoped everyone got clear in time because there was no reversing course at this point.

When he landed, the resulting shockwave of force shattered the nearby popcorn carts, carnival buildings, and tents, and set off every car alarm in the nearby parking lot, possibly as far as Parkside Boulevard itself.

In the wake of the crashed-and-burned Ferris wheel, Stardust breathed heavily and wished he could wipe his brow beneath his helmet. The magical fire had burned hotter than his environmental systems were prepared for.

It was then he noticed the circle of broken mirrors floating around him as he stood in the crater, each one reflecting a different Stardust. Like in the dream, all twenty of them glared at him, and he could see their respective suits powering up. Behind the mirrors, the hypnotist who'd put him into the dream stood unmoving and watchful, despite her blindness.

"Are you doing the magic whammy thing on me again?" Stardust asked. "Because that is so not cool."

The blind woman regarded him with an empty stare, her expression a little sad.

"At least I have my armor this time," he said with a very short-lived smile as the Stardust doppelgangers leaped out of the mirrors and attacked him from all sides.

Wild Kat had thought her friend Simon was unique. Known to the denizens of Cobalt City as Mister Grey, his fate was to live eternally as cremated ash, in a ghostly human form. It was not a common occurrence, and she had expected to go the rest of her life without experiencing it again. She was disappointed yet not surprised for the carnival to try and prove her wrong.

As she turned her eyes to watch the unfolding drama of Stardust fighting the flying Ferris wheel, Wild Kat was momentarily struck by how the wheel reminded her of the flaming wheels described by Ezekiel in the Old Testament and the wheel chandelier in Hildesheim Cathedral in German. It was only razor-honed senses that drew her attention to the scent of grave dust. She glanced down to see ash swirling around her feet and thought, for the briefest of moments, that Mister Grey had joined their cause.

But even ash had distinctive scents, particularly when her olfactory senses were overclocked as they were. Behind the ash, she detected a hint of something unfamiliar but undeniably floral. Wild Kat leaped from the grasping, smoky tendrils and landed ten feet away to look back at where she had been standing. A shape was coalescing there, a decrepit old man with hungry eyes.

This mysterious finger reached out for her. The thin arm shot across the gap between them, his dusty talons clawing at her nose and mouth, demanding entrance. Wild Kat clamped her mouth closed and exhaled sharply through her nose. A flying Ferris wheel might be out of her pay grade, but this, this she could deal with. She cartwheeled back and fixed her ghoulish target with a come-hither smile.

Wild Kat made certain not to run so fast that she lost the ashen specter, and spared several glances over her shoulder as she led him deep into the area of the kiddie rides. Having just raced through the area pursued by the murderous marionettes, she knew exactly what she wanted. She couldn't suppress her smile at the colorful shape looming ahead of her. However dark the

Carnaval Pomme D'or may be, you didn't make it in this business anymore without a bouncy house.

Sliding to a stop against the inflated rubber base, she paced herself with a quick three-count before turning around to face her pursuer. He hurled towards her, seemingly tireless, but more cloud than man at the moment. Wild Kat felt the thrum of the powerful fans used to keep the bouncy house inflated as she placed her palms upon the candy-colored structure.

As the ghastly old man figure pounced, Wild Kat trampolined through the bouncy house with all claws out. A hiss of air signaled the collapse of the rubberized structure behind her.

The massive gust of wind fragmented the dust man into a whirling storm, too shapeless to act as he blew away. Wild Kat didn't fool herself that he was gone for good. Simon had recovered from worse. But it would take time, and right now she could use one less person trying to attack her.

"Good help is so difficult to find," said a thickly accented woman's voice from the shadows of the collapsing bouncy house. "But I suppose congratulations are in order. You have forced me to become involved."

Wild Kat smelled that same unidentifiable floral scent, though much stronger. "Ah, are you this management I've been hearing so much about?"

A woman slithered into view, skin darker than the depths of the abyss, snake eyes daring Wild Kat to lock gaze upon them. Her lower torso was that of a giant serpent. "That is merely one title that fits," the snake woman said. She began circling Wild Kat to the left. "Mother of monsters is another. But I prefer my name: Lilith."

"If I had a dollar for every hopped up bint who called herself Lilith," Wild Kat began. The rest of her speech was cut short by the snake woman's attack. Much to her angry surprise, her foe struck quickly enough to sink long fangs into Wild Kat's left shoulder. She could only assume they were poisonous. They always were in cases like this.

The so-named Lilith pulled back and licked a drop of blood from her fangs. Her smile of satisfaction only stoked Wild Kat's rage. With a roar that sounded more slurred than was comforting, the fray was well and truly joined.

The tent had been larger on the inside than looks would indicate, spiraling down through the earth and into darkness. Kara, Snowflake, and Malenfant travelled down through the dark tunnels, their path guided by a phosphorescent light on the end of a screwdriver held by Kara and Snowflake's fish-shaped pocket flashlight. The twin light sources illuminated an unassuming man in a rumpled olive-green suit blocking their path. He was in his indeterminate middle-years, wearing a bored smile.

"Hello, Louis," he said. "I don't suppose you'll take a minute and talk this through?"

"John," Malenfant said without a note of surprise in his voice. "Of course they would send you. Ladies and gentlemen, allow me to introduce Unfortunate John."

Kara raised an eyebrow. "You know this guy?"

"We've met," John smiled. His eyes didn't move from Louis, as if he hadn't noticed the guns in the hands of Kara and Snowflake.

"In dreams," Louis said. "Why leave that part out, John?" He turned to his companions. "John visited me with some regularity in dreams when I was younger. More naive, I suppose," he returned his gaze to Unfortunate John. "But I didn't trust you then. I won't trust you now. And if my companions have any sense they won't trust you either."

A croaking laughter came from John's direction, though his lips never moved. John's smile turned apologetic. "You'll forgive us if we find that...amusing."

Snowflake leaned closer to Malenfant and whispered the question, "The hell is going on? Can I shoot this guy?"

Louis Malenfant didn't bother to whisper his reply. "Shooting John won't help. He has moved beyond such concerns centuries ago. Anyway, he isn't here to stop us, are you John? Or do you prefer your...older name?"

The smile vanished from the other man's face. "John will do. Kara, Snowflake, how well do you know this man? Pretty well, I would imagine, to follow him here," he paused long enough to let his gaze fall on both of Malenfant's companions. "The Carnaval Pomme D'or is home to many who could find no safe home elsewhere. But that doesn't matter to you, or to him. I know that. And I also know how this all ends. So Louis is right and true about one thing, at least. I am not here to stop you."

As Unfortunate John walked past them on his way out of the tent, Snowflake and Kara's eyes were drawn to the malformed face riding low upon the back of oracle's skull. The darkly glittering eyes that peeked from a crooked brow-like fold winked at them. "We won't stop you," the twisted mouth at the base of the skull croaked. "But you will wish we had."

John passed from their sight, lost quickly to the darkness. A nervous glance passed between the two gun-wielding heroes. Louis Malenfant pushed onwards. With only a second hesitation, they followed him soundlessly into the belly of the beast.

Stardust could barely remember a time when he wasn't blasting the holy bejesus out of one of his mirror-summoned doppelgangers. Some wore armor almost medieval in design, with weapons that pulsed with golden energy. Some piled onto him with armor so advanced Jaccob was distracted by his desire to reverse-engineer it.

It was like fighting a hydra, which brought back singularly unpleasant memories. With every fake Stardust he dropped, two more took its place. He had tried to call Wild Kat for assistance, but received no reply short of feral growls and grunts. Stardust could only assume she was as busy as he was. Exhaustion slipped in through the cracks of his battered and bruised body, and he began to let the slightest shred of doubt enter his mind that maybe this time he had bitten off more than he could chew.

If he survived the experience, Jaccob would never let himself live it down. He was used to beating himself up, but to have it done in such a literal and public manner was humiliating.

A faint tinkling sound caught Jaccob's attention. Several more followed, and he realized that fewer Stardusts were surrounding him. He even got his first clear look at the blind hypnotist since the fight had started, reaching out to stop Lumien from shattering the final mirror. The robot ignored her and swung a massive, brass fist. More glass shattered, and a swirl of silvered dust rained down upon the blind hypnotist. With a shriek, she collapsed.

Lumien's head spun on its neck mount, the giant lens in the center of the head contracting in recognition.

"Thanks, Lumien."

"Of course," Kara's companion said before locking in place. His lights went dead, and he became as useful as a giant, steampunk bookend.

A tall man in a black suit and a turban the color of blood stepped between them. Stardust raised his hands, ready to fire a starbolt but the ringmaster was too fast. He surged toward Stardust, caught him by the throat, and lifted him into the air without effort.

"I seem to be unable to move or see," Lumien said with an unnerving note of concern for a robot. "Stardust? What is happening?"

Stardust struggled, but the ringmaster was impossibly strong. The boss had come to play.

"You," the ringmaster said to Stardust, "have been particularly annoying today." He made a dismissive flicking gesture with his hand, and Stardust's armor ripped off his body in a storm of shrapnel. It left a sweaty, bruised man in its wake, who sagged in the ringmaster's grasp.

"Man, I hate magic," Jaccob said.

The heart of the carnival pulsed before them, a dark, mercurial form as large as Kara's van that hovered in the stale air. The ground beneath them was pale, fleshy, and sucked at their feet as they stared in a moment of abject horror. Though it had no eyes, they could feel it watching them with seething hatred. And they felt their heartbeats syncing up with it.

Deep in their core, it whispered to them, promising their deepest desires.

"It's a lie," Malenfant said, though his voice shook. "This being can give us nothing."

"But," Snowflake whispered. "That's a lot of girls in the hot tub with me. What if it isn't a lie?"

"I...no, I think Malenfant's right. A bigger tower than Starcom seems a bit preposterous."

"Really?" Snowflake said, disbelief fighting with fear in his voice. "Penis envy?"

"I...um...what?" Kara sputtered.

"Now is not the time for shenanigans," Malenfant snapped. "We must destroy this before it causes any further damage."

"Is that really what you want?" a voice said out of the darkness. It was ageless, but vaguely feminine. "Is that your true motivation? A noble protection of the mortals of this iteration?"

Malenfant blinked slowly, as if picturing his ideal world on the back of his eyelids. "So, you claim to be able to see into my heart? Look deeply, then and tell me what you see."

The claustrophobic confines took on a shiver of panic, invisible walls speeding towards them with the intensity of a freight train. Carried upon that, a scent of a dead lake and dusty, sun-baked stone, incongruous in the depths of the cave. Malenfant, if he truly was still Louis Malenfant, seemed to be growing in stature, a curved helm of bone manifesting upon his brow.

"Yes, I imagine it's been a while since you've had to face an equal," Malenfant said, his voice deeper. "To answer your question, think of it as less noble and more enlightened self-interest. This is my world, and I dislike interference."

Stardust was doing the math on exactly how long he could survive if his throat was well and truly crushed. He had reflexively taken a deep breath as the ringmaster lunged at him, so he figured he might have a good minute or so once that impossibly strong fist closed the rest of the way. He was thankful for the distracting tornado of Wild Kat and some kind of snake woman wrapped in a grapple that came crashing through the nearby debris of the Haunted Tunnel of Love.

As Stardust watched, Wild Kat rolled to the top and connected with a savage rake of claws across the throat of her opponent. It was enough of a distraction that the ringmaster dropped the now virtually naked and powerless Stardust to the churned earth.

The Ringmaster sounded unperturbed. "When Lilith regrows her throat, I will present your pelt to her as a treasure."

Wild Kat looked more weary than concerned. She extracted herself from the now limp coils. Stardust wasn't sure, but her voice sounded thick and slurred. "Seriously, did they get a bulk deal on lunatics when they staffed this carnival?"

From where he lay, Stardust saw the crumpled form of the blind hypnotist. He grit his teeth with determination and stood. His first step was shaky, his second less so. He tapped the ringmaster on the shoulder. "I'm not done with you yet," he said as the cocksure ringmaster turned.

Stardust's fist connected with the tip of the other man's pointed chin with so much force that it lifted him from the ground and sent the turban rolling on the ground. The fact that the ringmaster was bald beneath the red turban gave Stardust no small amount of satisfaction.

"Nicely done," Wild Kat said cheerfully.

"I am not my armor," Stardust answered with a touch less cheer. "But I wish I had it on when I punched him. I think I broke my hand."

From within the yellowed caul of the larger shape of the King in Yellow, Louis turned to wink at Kara and Snowflake. Time slowed around them until the scene was frozen in one, terrifying, crystalline moment. "I don't imagine this will confuse the carnival for long. I suggest you start shooting when you get the chance."

The ground lurched beneath their feet as time sped back up with a jolt. Snowflake, in a panic, fired off his laser at the ceiling, and the fleshy ground beneath them quivered. Kara aimed for the form in the air, and her shot had a similar but more potent impact. The panda, reclaiming a bit of reason, slid the beam of the laser down across the room and also aimed for the heart. With both the zap guns and the laser focusing on the same target, the dark mass began to shrink, while a black steam rose from the tumorous heart. When it was the size of a bowling ball, it seemed to fold in upon itself. Something inhuman screamed in the distance, and then it was gone.

An uneasy silence filled the cavern.

"Snowflake?" Kara said, her voice trembling. "Why did we give you the laser? You managed to miss the broadside of a barn."

Snowflake's voice squeaked a few times before words came out. "I'll have you know I'm an excellent marksman when I'm not peeing my pants."

Kara's laugh was brief and mirthless.

"No. Seriously. We should probably find a towel before I sit in your van again," Snowflake added.

Louis said nothing. His eyes were focused on the space where the heart had been moments before. His thin lips were pursed as if he had just tasted a rancid olive at a fancy dinner party and was uncertain of the protocol on spitting it out. "That was…unexpected. I suggest we leave quickly while we still have an exit."

Snowflake was surprised that his eyes could get any larger than they were already. "What do you mean no exit?"

Kara shook her head as she led the jog back up the tunnel towards freedom. "You didn't really think were still in a tent did you?"

Snowflake sound a bit defensive. "Maybe?"

"You need to watch some Doctor Who," Kara answered, never breaking stride. The others pushed to keep up.

Jaccob nursed his hand as Lumien sprang back to life. Wild Kat made her way quickly over to the others as paper bags, torn posters, and other garbage blew around them. The Carnaval Pomme D'or was vanishing around them like startled sea coral, pulling back into the protection of its hardened exterior. They didn't know where it was going. But they felt the change in the air. The carnival had been hurt. And now it was gone.

Wild Kat kicked through the debris toward him. "Have you seen the others?"

Lumien's head went up. "There they are," he pointed toward Kara and Snowflake.

"Where's Louis?" Wild Kat asked them.

"He was here," Snowflake said. He hugged the laser to his ample front as he surveyed the empty park. "Do I have to give this back now?"

"Yes!" they all answered him.

"Ah, hell," said the unabashed panda man, "let's go get a beer."

Louis gathered up the discarded paper fortunes, the tattered posters, the ticket stubs, and other bits that the Carnaval

Pomme D'or left behind. He dropped his notebook with its carefully written analysis of the carnival's nature on top. Then he lit the whole pile, watching the flames flare through a spectrum of colors not visible to normal human eyes.

He removed a scrap of paper from his pocket. It was a fortune, written in Latin. A parting gift from Unfortunate John. He words made no more sense on the tenth reading than they did on the first. He crumpled the paper slip and made to toss it onto the fire with the rest. He hesitated, unfolded the slip and read it one more time.

"Nonsense," he said aloud to the crackle and pop of the cleansing fire.

Without a further thought he let the clearly mistaken prophetic warning burn away from the world. He knew what he was. He didn't need Unfortunate John or Juno or whatever he called himself muddying those waters.

He knew his fate. The King in Yellow had seen to that. He was not now, nor would it ever be, any kind of hero.

He left before the fire burned to ash, otherwise he might have seen the few scraps that refused to burn.

Carnival Heart was a joint collaborative effort, written by Erik Scott de Bie, Rosemary Jones, Dawn Vogel, and Jeremy Zimmerman, and guided by notes from Nathan Crowder.

Epilogue
Matt Adams

A faceless, hulking monster of a man ambled up to a city in rural France with picture tubes tucked under his arms and a backpack full of fliers.

Patiently, he hung the fliers on various buildings around the city, moving from location to location to herald the coming of *Le Carnaval Pomme D'or*.

No matter how many posters he put up, he never ran out. No matter how much tape he used, he never needed more. No matter how many staples the work required, he never needed to refill his staple gun.

The carnival marched on toward its next stop.

The featured performer for this tour: Harrigan the Magnificent, Master of the Psychic Arts.

Cobalt City is the super-hero shared universe line of anthologies and novels from Timid Pirate Publishing. Many of the characters presented in *Cobalt City Dark Carnival* have appeared in those pages. To read their ongoing adventures, we have provided a convenient listing of other Cobalt City titles.

Further Reading

Chanson Noir (Protectorate Volume 1)
By Nathan Crowder

The Protectorate saga begins here! There are other worlds besides our own, stacked in an unfolding coil of possibilities. The Queen of the Black Sigh rules over her own world as the timeless avatar of physical decay. But her palace is also her prison, for the artifact she needs to breach the veil between worlds has been lost to the ages. If someone were to uncover her Obsidian Mirror, the gateway would be open to her, and countless realities would fall before her insatiable hunger. And when the mirror is uncovered, it falls to The Protectorate, heroes of Cobalt City to stop her.
Featuring: Stardust, Doctor Shadow, Knockabout, Mister Grey, Wild Kat, and Louis Malenfant.

Cobalt City Blues (Protectorate Volume 2)
By Nathan Crowder

Dead over seventy years and acting the part of super-hero Mister Grey, Simon wants nothing more than a return to some semblance of his old life. Even if it risks the safety of his friends and fellow heroes in the Protectorate. Book Two of the Protectorate series, Cobalt City Blues is an epic novel of alternate realities, loss, redemption, jazz, super-heroes, and what it means to be human.
Featuring: Stardust, Doctor Shadow, Knockabout, Libertine, Mister Grey, Wild Kat, Snowflake, and Louis Malenfant.

Cobalt City Christmas
Edited by Nathan Crowder

Unwrap a bundle of super-powered adventure for the holidays, including tasty tales from storytellers both new and established. Join Nathan Crowder, Angel Leigh McCoy, Rosemary Jones, Jeremy Zimmerman, and Nicole Burns for a dose of fun and festivities that will keep you cheering for the holidays year round. *Featuring: Stardust, Knockabout, Kara Sparx & Lumien, Mister Grey, Wild Kat, and Snowflake.*

Cobalt City Timeslip
Edited by Caroline Dombrowski

Diving into the history of Cobalt City, this time-spanning collection is the super-hero anthology you've been waiting for. A perfect introduction into the world of cape and cowl fiction featuring original stories by Nathan Crowder, Rosemary Jones, Erik Scott de Bie, Jeremy Zimmerman, Dawn Vogel, and others.

About Timid Pirate Publishing

Founded in Seattle in 2010, Timid Pirate Publishing believes that heroes walk among us, although most don't wear capes. You never know when your own inner hero will awaken. We believe that joy and inspiration are everywhere, and once found, should be shared. To that end, we share stories that inspire and delight, and that broaden the world of possibilities while entertaining. In short: Adventures Unlimited.

We firmly believe in treating people, both real and fictional, with compassion. That goes for all people. Even the ones we disagree with. Sometimes especially the ones we disagree with.

Most of all, we subscribe to a spirit of adventure—to finding the stories untold and the authors who forge their own path rather than follow the fickle whims of the "market."

Timid Pirate Publishing provides free, original stories online at their website www.timidpirate.com, as well as the award-winning audio drama "Cobalt City: Adventures Unlimited."

Find us on Twitter @TimidPirate, "like" us on Facebook, or subscribe to our monthly newsletter for all the news and updates on coming projects, appearances, and special events.

www.ingramcontent.com/pod-product-compliance
Lightning Source LLC
Chambersburg PA
CBHW020133180626
46810CB00004B/1530